KT-393-463

Marty and her big sister Melissa couldn't be more different – and they just don't get along. Marty is a messy tomboy and loves animals, snuggling up in her cosy, comfy den and drawing her comics – especially her favourite character, the brilliant Mighty Mart. So living with pink, girlie, super-annoying Melissa has never been easy.

But things are about to get much worse. When Mum's new dress-making business takes off, she needs a spare room in the house to use for her sewing. For the first time ever, Marty and Melissa have to share a room – and the girls are soon fighting every single day.

But when an everyday argument goes horribly wrong, will Marty realize just how much her big sister really means to her?

www.**kids**at**randomhouse**.co.uk

ALSO AVAILABLE BY JACQUELINE WILSON

Published in Corgi Pups, for beginner readers:
THE DINOSAUR'S PACKED LUNCH
THE MONSTER STORY-TELLER

Published in Young Corgi, for newly confident readers:
LIZZIE ZIPMOUTH
SLEEPOVERS

Available from Doubleday / Corgi Yearling Books:
BAD GIRLS
THE BED AND BREAKFAST STAR
BEST FRIENDS
BIG DAY OUT
BURIED ALIVE!
CANDYFLOSS
THE CAT MUMMY
CLEAN BREAK
CLIFFHANGER
COOKIE
THE DARE GAME
THE DIAMOND GIRLS
DOUBLE ACT
DOUBLE ACT (PLAY EDITION)
GLUBBSLYME
HETTY FEATHER
THE ILLUSTRATED MUM
JACKY DAYDREAM
LILY ALONE
LITTLE DARLINGS
THE LONGEST WHALE SONG
THE LOTTIE PROJECT
MIDNIGHT
THE MUM-MINDER
MY SECRET DIARY
MY SISTER JODIE
SAPPHIRE BATTERSEA
SECRETS
STARRING TRACY BEAKER
THE STORY OF TRACY BEAKER
THE SUITCASE KID
VICKY ANGEL
THE WORRY WEBSITE

Collections:
THE JACQUELINE WILSON COLLECTION
includes THE STORY OF TRACY BEAKER *and*
THE BED AND BREAKFAST STAR
JACQUELINE WILSON'S DOUBLE-DECKER
includes BAD GIRLS *and* DOUBLE ACT
JACQUELINE WILSON'S SUPERSTARS
includes THE SUITCASE KID *and* THE LOTTIE PROJECT

Available from Doubleday / Corgi Books, for older readers:
DUSTBIN BABY
GIRLS IN LOVE
GIRLS UNDER PRESSURE
GIRLS OUT LATE
GIRLS IN TEARS
KISS
LOLA ROSE
LOVE LESSONS

Join the official Jacqueline Wilson fan club at
www.jacquelinewilson.co.uk

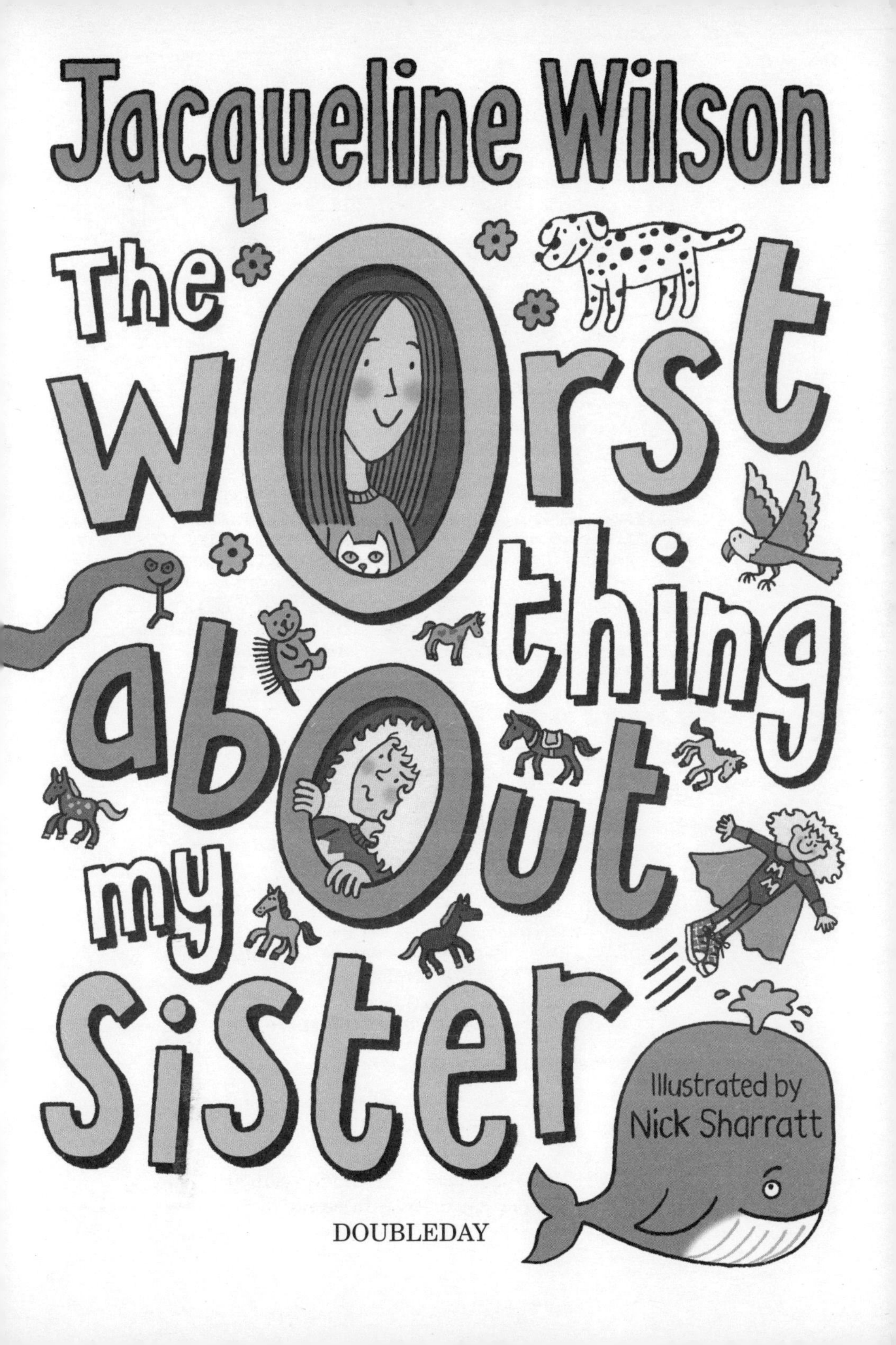
Jacqueline Wilson
The worst thing about my sister
Illustrated by
Nick Sharratt
M
M
DOUBLEDAY

THE WORST THING ABOUT MY SISTER
A DOUBLEDAY BOOK 978 0 385 61893 9
TRADE PAPERBACK 978 0 857 53100 1

Published in Great Britain by Doubleday,
an imprint of Random House Children's Books
A Random House Group company

This edition published 2012

3 5 7 9 10 8 6 4 2

The Random House Group Limited supports the Forest Stewardship Council
(FSC®), the leading international forest certification organization. Our books
carrying the FSC label are printed on FSC®-certified paper. FSC is the only
forest certification scheme endorsed by the leading environmental
organizations, including Greenpeace. Our paper procurement policy
can be found at www.randomhouse.co.uk/environment.

Set in 14/19pt New Century Schoolbook

RANDOM HOUSE CHILDREN'S BOOKS
61–63 Uxbridge Road, London W5 5SA

www.**kids**at**randomhouse**.co.uk
www.**totallyrandombooks**.co.uk
www.**randomhouse**.co.uk

Addresses for companies within The Random House Group Limited
can be found at: www.randomhouse.co.uk/offices.htm

THE RANDOM HOUSE GROUP Limited Reg. No. 954009

A CIP catalogue record for this book is available
from the British Library.

Printed and bound in Great Britain by Clays Ltd, St Ives plc

In memory of Molly
and her sister Isabella –
who loved each other dearly

The worst thing about my sister is she's such a *girl*. Well, I'm a girl too, but I'm not a dinky-pinky, silly-frilly girlie girl. Think cupcakes and cuddly teddies and charm bracelets – that's Melissa.

She leaves a little pink trail around the house – sparkly slides and ribbons and notebooks.

You breathe in her revolting scent long after she's gone off to hang out at her friends' houses. She's not allowed to wear real perfume yet, but she's got this rose hand cream that smells really strongly. She doesn't just rub it on her hands, she smoothes it in all over, so she's always slightly slippery.

Her lips shine too, because she's forever smearing on lip gloss. She's not really supposed to wear make-up yet either, only for play, but she's got a big plastic bag patterned with pink kittens, and it's crammed full of eye shadows and mascara and blusher. It used to be just Mum's old stuff, but now Melissa spends half her pocket money in Superdrug.

When Melissa was in the loo, I crept into her ultra pink and fluffy bedroom to borrow a pen as mine had all run out. I couldn't find her school bag – it must have been downstairs by the computer – so in desperation I looked in her plastic make-up bag. I found a brand-new eye pencil with a perfect point and its own cool little sharpener.

I went back to my Marty Den, sat on my top bunk, and started drawing an amazing new adventure of Mighty Mart. I didn't mean to use a lot of the pencil. I was just going to do a quick sketch. But then I had this great idea of giving Mighty Mart giant springs in her feet, so she could jump – *b-o-i-n-g* – over rooftops and lampposts and trees. Drawing all these astonishing feats took up three full pages in my sketch-book – and most of Melissa's eye pencil.

Then Melissa poked her nose into my Marty Den, rabbiting on about some missing hairbrush. (I'd experimented gluing it onto the back of a little mangled teddy, turning him into a pretty cool porcupine called Percy.) She failed to spot him snuffling for ants under my bunk beds, but she *did* see the stub of her eye pencil in my hot little hand.

'You horrible thieving *pig*!' she gasped. 'That pencil was brand-new – and there's hardly any left now.'

'Well, it's not very good value then, is it?' I said, a little unwisely. Maybe I should have said sorry – but she did call me a pig. Not that I actually dislike pigs. I think they're very cute, and I love scratching their backs with a stick when we go to the children's zoo.

Anyway, do you know what Melissa *did*? She ripped all three pages out of my book and tore them to shreds. I couldn't *believe* she could be so hateful. I mean, she could always buy another silly pencil. I might even have paid half out of my pocket money. But I'd spent two whole *hours* drawing Mighty Mart, and now she was just confetti on the carpet. So I thumped Melissa in the chest. And she slapped my face. And then we were rolling around on the floor, shoving and screaming.

I'm a much better fighter than Melissa, but she scratches with her pointy fingernails. I'm fast and furious and I know how to punch properly, but Melissa is a lot bigger than me.

Perhaps *that's* the worst thing about my sister. She's two and a half years older, and no matter how hard I try I can never catch up.

I'd have still beaten her, I'm sure of it.

If we'd been left to our own devices, Melissa would have ended up as pink pulp, but Mum came running out of her bedroom and barged into my Marty Den to stop us.

'What are you *doing*? Stop it at *once*, Martina and Melissa! You know you are absolutely strictly forbidden to fight. You're not little guttersnipes, you're *girls*.'

She pulled us apart and stood us on our feet. 'How dare you!' she hissed. 'Especially today, when Mrs Evans and Alisha are in my bedroom and can hear everything. Alisha's such a sweet little girl too. You'd never catch *her* fighting.'

'Alisha's such a wuss she couldn't punch her way out of a paper bag,' I said.

Alisha is in my class at school and I absolutely can't stand her. She sucks up to Katie and Ingrid, the two really mean, scary girls. She gives them crisps and chocolates so they won't pick on her. She *loves* it if they pick on someone else. Like me.

I didn't invite her round to our house. As if! She came round with her mother because *our* mother was making her a party dress. Mum was starting to become *famous* for making terrible frilly frocks with smocking and embroidery and a thousand and one prickly net petticoats. She used to make matching dresses for Melissa and me when we were really little. I used to scream my head off and keep my arms pressed tight against my sides to stop her putting one on me. Melissa used to *like* hers, and would flounce around swishing her skirts in an especially sickening way. Nowadays even she has seen sense and says smocked dresses are babyish and embarrassing, the exact opposite of cool.

But our dresses became a terrible talking point in our neighbourhood, and other mums still want to inflict frills on their little kids, so Mum's wondering if she can make a little money out of making dresses. She's busy designing party dresses and bridesmaids' dresses and confirmation dresses. So busy she doesn't always have time to look at what *we're* wearing. When we're not stuck in our rubbish red-and-white check school uniform, Melissa hitches up her skirts and wears tight tops and puts socks in her training bra. She thinks she looks much older, practically a teenager. She is *so* pathetic.

I wear my comfy jeans and my POW! T-shirt and my tartan Converse boots. I wear them again and again because they're my favourite clothes, so I don't see the point of wearing any others.

'Look at the *state* of you!' said Mum. She shook us both

and then continued to hang onto my T-shirt, peering at it. 'For goodness' sake, Martina, this T-shirt's filthy!'

'It's just a little dribble of orange juice when I laughed at the wrong time at supper. It's so weird when it all comes spouting out of your nose.'

'That was *days* ago! You know perfectly well you're supposed to put on a clean T-shirt every day. Have I got to stand over you and dress you like a baby?' said Mum.

Melissa sniggered, which was a stupid move.

'I'm very shocked at *you*, Melissa. You really ought to know better. You're the eldest. What were you thinking of, fighting with your little sister?'

'She used up nearly all my eye pencil, Mum, scribbling her silly cartoons.'

'Mighty Mart is a comic strip, not a cartoon. And you tore it all up, and I spent *ages* on it.'

'As if any of this *matters*,' said Mum.

'Now, tidy yourselves up. Melissa, you go downstairs and get the pizzas out of the freezer. Martina, change that T-shirt *now*. And both of you, stop showing me up in front of Mrs Evans.'

As if on cue, Mrs Evans started calling from Mum's bedroom: 'I think you've made Alisha's dress a little on the skimpy side, Mrs Michaels. She can scarcely breathe!'

Mum rolled her eyes. 'I'm so sorry, Mrs Evans. Don't worry – I can always let it out a little at the seams,' she called back.

'And I'm not sure the hem's straight. It's difficult to tell, what with your bed being in the way of your wardrobe mirror – but it seems to ride right up in the front,' Mrs Evans moaned.

'That's because of Alisha's great fat stomach!' I muttered.

'Martina!' said Mum – but she was trying not to laugh. She hurried off and left Melissa and me glaring at each other.

'Tell-tale,' I said.

'You told too. And that eye pencil cost four ninety-nine.'

'Then you're bonkers wasting your pocket money like that.'

'It's going to be *your* pocket money! You're going to buy me a new one.'

'No, *you're* going to buy me a new drawing pad seeing as you've ruined this one. Now get out of my den. You're not allowed in here – can't you read?' I said.

I had stuck a very clear notice on my door.

'You've got a cheek, seeing as you went into *my* room to nick my eye pencil. You're such a waste of space, Marty. If only I had a *proper* sister. Why do you always have to be so *weird*?'

Melissa flounced off down to the kitchen. I sat biting my nails, thinking up a wonderful new sequence for Mighty Mart where she turns ultra weird overnight, with prickles all over and great fangs – all the better for *biting* people. But I couldn't draw her because I didn't have anything to draw *with*, as Melissa had reclaimed her eye pencil and all my pens had either run out or exploded. There was a very inky corner of my school bag, especially the bit where I'd stuffed my PE kit, but I wasn't in the mood for investigating it.

I didn't change my T-shirt either. My clothes were mostly cast-offs from Melissa, dreadful limp pink things with bunnies and kittens. I *like* bunnies and kittens, but not as cutesy-pie pictures on T-shirts. I'd have given anything for a proper pet, though not necessarily something fluffy. A real porcupine would be ultra-cool. Or a turtle who could live in the bath. Or a hyena that laughed at my jokes – though I'd probably have to keep him in a cage in the garden. I'm not sure you could ever house-train a hyena. I imagined it savaging Mum's silks and satins and squatting on Alisha's lilac party dress. I did a hyena laugh myself going across the landing.

'*Martina!*' Mum hissed, putting her head out of the door.

I saw Alisha's mum behind her, eyes all beady, and Alisha herself in her knickers. She really *did* have a big tummy.

'Could you just *behave*? And change that dreadful T-shirt!' said Mum. She pulled that face that means *Do as I say this instant or you'll be for it!*

I put the kitten T-shirt on back to front so I couldn't see the cutesy furry face, and

went stomping downstairs. I put my hand over my mouth because I badly wanted to let out another hyena laugh and I knew this would not be a good idea.

I avoided the kitchen, where Melissa was juggling pizzas and clattering cutlery, laying the trays for supper, doing her *I'm the good big sister* act. I went into the front room to check on Dad.

It isn't really the front room any more. It's become Dad's travel agency office. Dad used to have a real travel agent's shop down that street near Sainsbury's, but he had to give it up because the lease was too expensive and he didn't make enough money any more.

He set up as a travel agent in our front room instead. We went to Ikea to buy some shelving, but they didn't have the sort Dad wanted, so we bought our own MDF, which was much more fun. Dad was Carpenter-in-Chief and I was his Number One Assistant when it came to painting all the planks white. We had to do it outside in the garden because Mum was terrified I'd tip the paint over, but I didn't spill a drop! When they were dry I helped Dad fix all the shelves in place – and they looked terrific.

Melissa helped him display all his travel books and brochures on our beautiful new shelves, and Mum framed all these posters of mountains and lakes and white sandy beaches and hung them on the walls. Dad set up his computer, and there he was, all ready for the rush of customers. But nobody came.

Well, a *few* clients came – really old ones who couldn't use a computer to book their own holidays. Dad fixed up a weekend in Paris here, ten days in Tenerife there, but for the most part he sat all by himself, scrolling down all the amazing holiday offers on his screen. Sometimes he switched off and simply gazed at the mountains and the lakes and the beaches on the walls.

We didn't have enough money now to go away on holiday ourselves, even though Dad was trying his hardest to support the family and be successful. We just had Mum's money from her sewing and working as a school secretary. *Our* school secretary. It was a bit odd being sent to the office with the register and seeing your own mum behind the desk. We were meant to call her Mrs Michaels there, but I didn't always remember.

'Hey, Dad,' I said.

'Hey, Marty,' he said, sighing.

I stood right in front of him and tickled

his head. He sighed again, but he reached out and tickled *my* head.

'Hey, Curlynob,' we said in unison.

It's our little ritual, to show we're mates. Dad has very fair frizzy curls, even though his hair is cut really short. I'd give anything to have *my* hair cut really short but Mum won't let me. I have to have it loose to my shoulders at home and in awful little plaits at school. My curly hair drives me mad – but I love being like Dad.

Melissa has very straight mouse-brown hair. She never *says*, but I think she'd give anything to have my fair curls. Don't get the idea that I'm *pretty*, though! I've got a snub nose and a pointy chin, and go freckly in the summer.

I pulled a funny face now to try to make Dad laugh, because he was looking very sad. He chuckled politely, but it wasn't a real laugh.

'Hey, do you want to hear my hyena laugh?' I said, and I demonstrated.

'Oh, help, help, I'm fwightened!' said Dad, pretending to be little. 'There's a big bad hyena in the room and it's coming to get me!'

'The big bad hyena is in a spot of trouble, Dad,' I said. 'It scribbled with its sister's eye pencil, and then it got into a fight, and its mother got cross because that awful podgy Alisha Evans and her mum are up in our bedroom.'

'Oh Lord, I forgot they were coming. I think I might have left the bed all rumpled when I had a nap after lunch,' said Dad. He had lots of naps now because he didn't have anything else to do. 'I probably left my pyjamas out in a heap. Looks like I'm in a spot of bother too.'

'I wish Mum didn't get grumpy all the time,' I said.

'Now, now, your mum only gets cross because we're such a slobby pair and she's working very, very hard,' said Dad.

'*I've* been working very, very hard, Dad. I did three whole pages of Mighty Mart, only *somebody* came along and ripped them all up.'

'You're *my* Mighty Mart,' said Dad, and he pulled me onto his knee for a cuddle.

I snuggled up with my chin on his shoulder, staring at the posters on the wall. Mighty Mart would stomp all the way up that mountain in a matter of minutes, she'd swim across the lake like it was a duck pond, and then she'd lie on the white beach and let a whole team of little kids try to bury her in the sand.

Just when they thought they'd trapped her so she'd have to stay motionless like a monument for ever, she'd laugh and jump up and send them all scattering as she strode away in her giant Converse boots.

I was invited to Alisha's party! I didn't didn't didn't want to go. I couldn't stand Alisha and she couldn't stand me, but because my mum had made her dress I was given an invitation.

'I'm not going!' I said to Mum.

'Oh yes, you are,' Mum said firmly.

'Mum, I really really hate girlie parties.'

'Don't be silly, Martina,' said Mum.

'Can't Melissa go instead?'

'Alisha's *your* friend, dopey.'

'No she's not! She's just in my class at school. And I hate her.'

'You don't *hate* her, you maybe just don't like her very much,' said Mum.

'Exactly, so why should I have to go to her party if I don't like her very much. At all,' I said.

'Because . . . because I don't want to offend Mrs Evans,' said Mum.

'Why aren't you worried about offending *me*?' I said, stamping off to my Marty Den.

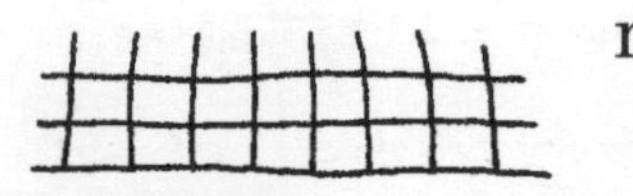

I wriggled right under my bunk beds into my dark, dusty lair. My Percy Porcupine was hiding there too. He prickled me, but I forgave him. I stroked his nose and fed him little balls of dust, and he wriggled and squiggled appreciatively. He said he didn't ever want to turn back into a hairbrush and half a teddy, which was just as well, as he was pretty grubby by now. So was I, but I didn't care.

I loved my bunk beds. I had begged for them year after year until Mum and Dad eventually gave in and bought me them for my birthday, when we still had lots of money.

I didn't share them with Melissa, of course. She had her own boring bed in her pink candyfloss bedroom. I shared with all *sorts* of friends, though I made sure I always had the top bunk. I didn't share with anybody *human*, though I had plans to invite my new friend Jaydene for a sleepover. She'd just started at my school and I liked her a lot. Meanwhile, I shared with my animals.

My absolute favourite (though don't tell the others) is Wilma Whale. She was on a duvet cover I found at a school jumble sale.

Mum wouldn't buy her for me because purple and turquoise wouldn't go with my red colour scheme – and she said she was hideous anyway. So *I* bought Wilma with my own pocket money. Mum made her lurk underneath my red-and-white checked duvet during the day, but at night I'd lie on Wilma and we'd swim to the bottom of the ocean, and then swoop up up up again and spout a fountain of water into the sunlight.

I also had Jumper, my big black and white Dalmatian dog. Dad won him for me at a fair. Jumper wasn't very good at lying down in a relaxed kind of way. His legs stuck straight down and he wouldn't cuddle. Still, he made a very good guard dog for my Marty Den. I also had

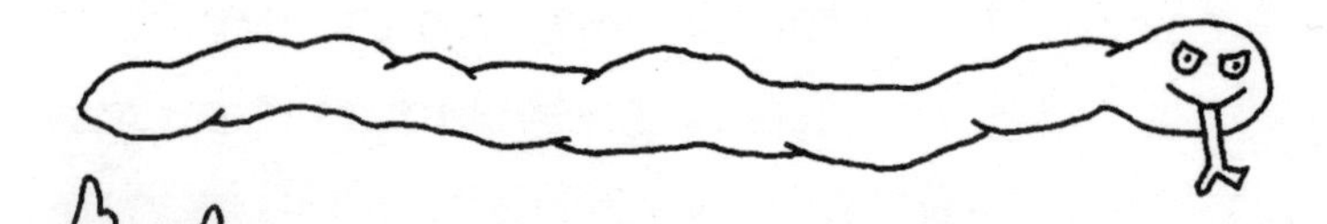

Basil the boa constrictor. I'd made him myself out of Mum's old tights and sewn a ferocious face at one end. Then there was Polly the parrot – she was cardboard, but very brightly coloured and fantastic at flying. I had an entire shoe box stable full of plastic horses as well, so the bottom bunk got very crowded.

Sometimes I made all my animals budge up so that Mighty Mart herself could sleep in the bottom bunk. She had to reduce her superpowers considerably to squeeze herself down to a suitable size, and even so her hands and feet stuck out right into my room, but that didn't matter a bit. She loved to laze on my bunk bed and tell me about all the exciting places she'd visited.

Occasionally, when I couldn't get to sleep, she'd lift me onto her shoulders the way Dad used to carry me when I was little, and we'd open up my bedroom window and fly out into the night together on a big adventure.

I wasn't up to any adventuring just now, lurking under my bunk beds in the dust. I decided I would hide there until the day *after* Alisha's party – but it was getting near supper time and Dad always went out for fish and chips on a Friday night. I heard the front door and then smelled a wonderful savoury chippy smell, and I couldn't contain myself.

I rushed downstairs without thinking. Mum grabbed hold of me and marched me right back up again just because I had grey dust all over me. Even in my hair actually. It did look a bit eerie, like

those men who paint themselves silver and then stand like statues down the shopping centre on Saturday. I wondered if I could have a shot at posing like a statue, because people gave them lots of money. I stood motionless in the bathroom for quite a while, practising. By the time I'd had a wash and brushed the fluff out of my hair my fish and chips were nearly cold.

'Goodness, who are you?' said Dad as I came into the living room. 'Now let me think . . . Didn't we once have another daughter besides Melissa? Long, long, ago. What was she called? Maisie? Matty?'

'It's me, *Marty*. Dad, don't be daft,' I said, tucking into my chips. I shook lots of tomato sauce on top. Red is my all-time favourite colour.

'Stop it, Martina, you're using half the bottle!' said Mum. 'Have you stopped sulking now?'

'Anyone would sulk if they were told they had to go to Alisha's party,' I said. I didn't like the way Mum was looking at me, her eyes squinting, her head peering this way and that.

Halfway through supper she went for her tape measure and started measuring me!

'Why are you doing that? Stop it!' I said.

'Hold still!' said Mum, moving the tape about.

'You're not going to make something for me, are you?' I asked, my voice croaky with fear. 'Oh, Mum, it's not a *dress*, is it?'

'I want you to look lovely at the party,' said Mum.

'But, *Mum* – not a dress! I can't wear a dress. *Nobody* wears dresses to parties nowadays.'

'Alisha does.'

'Yes, well, Alisha is so pathetic maybe she will. But no one else does, I swear. You wear just ordinary stuff – jeans and tops, maybe skirts sometimes, but never ever dresses. *Tell* her, Melissa. Even you wouldn't wear a dress to a party, would you?'

Melissa chewed a chip daintily, her eyes bright. 'I think it's a lovely idea, Mum. Marty needs a proper party dress – a really frilly one with smocking and embroidery – a *pink* party dress,' she said.

'Stop it!' I howled, almost in tears.

That's the worst thing about my sister. She never misses a chance to wind me up.

'Hey, hey, calm down, Curlynob. Melissa's only joking,' said Dad, putting his arm round me. He looked at Mum. 'And you're joking too, aren't you, Jan?'

'No I'm not! Stop making a silly fuss, Martina. I know you don't like pink, though it would really suit you. But I think I will go for blue – maybe a deep cornflower. I've seen some lovely silky stuff in the market.'

I moaned despairingly and started thumping my head on the table.

'Martina! Stop being so silly and melodramatic. Any other little girl would be absolutely thrilled at the idea of a lovely party dress. *You* would be, wouldn't you, Melissa?'

'Well . . .' I was in such deep despair that even my sister took pity on me. 'Actually, Mum, Marty's right – no one wears that sort of pretty dress to parties now. The dress you made for Alisha is lovely, but it's more like a bridesmaid's dress. She's going to look a bit weird if she wears it to her party. And Marty's going to look even weirder, trust me.'

'It's a *dance* party. It's being held at Alisha's dancing school. Alisha's mum told me all about it. It's going to be like a very junior prom.'

'*Dancing!* Oh, there won't be dancing, will there?' I said, even more horrified. 'Not pointy-toes, prancing-about ballet dancing? I *can't* go, Mum.'

I looked at Dad. 'Dad, please, I don't really have to go, do I? Imagine how you'd feel if *you* had to wear a silly dress and do ballet dancing.'

'Give the kid a break, Jan,' said Dad. 'You know what our Marty's like. Maybe other little girls would like it, but it'll be torture for her.'

'I think she'll probably enjoy herself when she gets there. And *she* won't have to do any dancing – though I wish she would. It would be so good for her – give her a little grace, instead of forever clumping about in those awful Converse boots. Ah! We'll obviously have to get you a proper pair of shoes for the party, unless your school ones will do. No – they'll spoil the whole effect.'

'Oh, Mum, if Marty's having new shoes can I have some too? I'd really like some heels, just little ones. All the other girls in my class have got really high-heeled shoes. I'm the only one going around in baby shoes with soles as flat as pancakes,' Melissa said.

'Don't *you* start, Melissa. You're not wearing high heels at your age. They're very bad for growing feet. And we can't afford for you to have another pair of shoes. I've only just bought you those silly furry boots you were so desperate to have.'

'They're *winter* boots. And it's not fair – why should Marty have new shoes when she doesn't even want them, especially if you say you can't afford to buy me any,' Melissa said, throwing down her knife and fork.

'Now, now, you womenfolk!' said Dad. 'Let's all just enjoy our fish and chips and

stop all this argy-bargy. Jan, for what it's worth, I think you've got your wires crossed. Marty doesn't want to go to a party, so it seems mad to force her. Then she won't need a new dress *or* shoes, so why not use the money you'd spend on them to give Melissa her heels – *little* ones. Simple.'

'Oh, Dad, yes!' Melissa and I said joyfully.

'It's not simple,' said Mum. She looked at Melissa and me. 'I'm sorry, girls. I *need* Marty to go to the party.'

'Why? Just because you don't want to upset Amanda Evans and her unfortunate podgy daughter?' said Dad.

‘I need someone looking pretty as a picture at that party,’ Mum said. ‘I’ve tried my best with Alisha’s dress, but it really doesn’t suit her, poor girl. But if I run up a little dress for Martina and tidy her up a bit *and* keep her clean, she’ll do me proud.’

‘I don’t want to!’ I protested bitterly.

‘She’ll act like a little model for me, don’t you see? Some of the other mothers might want *their* daughters to have a similar party dress. It would be really good for business,’ said Mum.

‘But – but you haven’t really *got* a proper business,’ said Dad.

‘Not yet – but I’d like one,’ said Mum. She paused. ‘And it would be a help.’

She said it very gently, but Dad flushed and looked miserable. Mum meant that he wasn’t earning any money from *his* business. It wasn’t his fault, he was really trying hard to make it a success. I couldn’t bear it when his face went all droopy like that. None of us could.

'I think these fish and chips have gone cold,' Mum said quickly. 'How about we leave them and I make us all pancakes instead?'

Mum's pancakes are our all-time favourite thing, though she doesn't often make them because she's too tired and too busy. It was a clever suggestion because we all three cheered up. Mum let us choose our own toppings. I had strawberry jam and sliced peach and chopped nuts and whirly cream. Then she gave us all a second pancake!

'It wouldn't be possible to have *thirds*, would it, Mum?' I said when I had cleared my plate twice over. I'd had to undo my jeans and I could barely move, but it still seemed worth asking, just in case.

'You don't want to end up looking like Alisha, do you?' said Mum, which shut me up quick.

I hoped that somehow or other Mum would forget all about the dreaded dress for Alisha's party. I sat up in bed that night drawing Mighty Mart swooping all over the city, going *zap-zap-zap* with her finger. All the people in the street and in their cars and at the windows of their houses had blank faces with open mouths because Mighty Mart had wiped their memories clean and they couldn't remember a single thing.

But she couldn't manage to wipe my mum's memory. She got started on the dreaded dress the very next day – and she bought me silly little blue pull-on satin slippers.

'Mum! They're like ballet shoes!' I moaned.

'They'll go beautifully with the blue silk. They were selling them cheap in the market. I got you a new pair of white socks too – *and* a new pair of knickers in case you leap about and disgrace me. All your underwear is *grey*!'

My face went grey too at the thought of this wretched party. Alisha was going on and on about it at school. She didn't invite my special friend Jaydene, the lucky thing. She *did* invite Katie and Ingrid, the worst girls in the class. The girls who pick on me. They whisper silly things about me and call me Freak and Weirdo. I don't give a fig – I can take care of myself. If I wanted to, I could zap them just like Mighty Mart. Still, I don't want to go to a *party* with them. Especially not wearing a frilly blue dress.

When Saturday morning came, I burrowed down under my red-and-white checked duvet *and* Wilma Whale. When I was simply roasting, I scribbled red crayon across my cheeks. Then I went padding into Mum and Dad's bedroom.

'Mum! Dad! I don't feel very well,' I said in a sad, croaking voice.

'Stop trying it on, Martina,' said Mum, without even opening her eyes.

'I'm *not* trying it on, I'm ill – *look*, I'm all flushed.'

Mum opened one eye and groaned. 'What have you *done*? It's going to take hours rubbing that red stuff off your face.'

'It's not red stuff. It's me! I've got a terrible fever. Feel my forehead. And yet I'm shaking too – see?' I said, quivering piteously.

'Come here and have a cuddle before you keel over,' Dad said, reaching out an arm.

I snuggled into bed between them, though Mum made me lie on my back so my cheeks wouldn't rub off on their pillows.

'You really don't want to go to this wretched party, do you, Curlynob?' said Dad, patting my head.

'It will be torture from beginning to end,' I declared dramatically, which made him chuckle. '*Especially* if I have to wear that blue monstrosity,' I added.

'Hey, hey, no need to be cheeky now. Your mum's spent ages making that dress, sewing till her hands are sore,' said Dad.

'I didn't ask her to,' I said.

'I can't wait to see you in it,' said Dad.

'So you can have a good laugh,' I mumbled.

'The laugh will be on you, Martina, because you're going to look lovely,' said Mum. 'Now, if you're staying in this bed, settle down and keep quiet while we all have a little doze.'

I wore my own POW! T-shirt and comfy jeans and tartan Converse boots all morning, but straight after lunch I had to go and have a bath, for goodness' sake, and then stand looking foolish in my new knickers and socks and silly little satin slippers while Mum brushed my curls until it felt as if I had grooves in my scalp. She wanted to stick a blue

ribbon in my hair, but thank goodness my curls were so springy it kept falling out, so she gave up on that idea.

The blue dress felt very slippery as she pulled it over my head. Maybe that would fall off too. But it stayed on, gripping me tight round my waist.

'It's a perfect fit,' Mum said.

She was whispering as if we were in a museum. She circled me as if *I* were an exhibit. Her eyes were shining.

'Oh, Martina!' she said. 'You really do look lovely, darling. See!' She took me gently by my blue silk shoulders and steered me in front of the mirror.

I looked *terrible*. I didn't look like me any more. I'd turned into some simpering soft ultra-girlie girl in the most elaborately awful silly-frilly dress. I looked like the crinoline lady in my great-gran's bathroom who keeps a spare toilet roll under her skirt.

'I can't go looking like this! They'll all laugh at me,' I said.

'You really are the giddy limit, Martina. You might at least say "Thank you, Mum." Any other girl would give their eye teeth to have a dress like this. Wait till Melissa sees you. Melissa! Melissa, come and look at Martina.'

Melissa came rushing into Mum and Dad's room. She took one look at me – and burst out laughing.

'You see!' I said, practically in tears.

'Melissa, stop it! Martina looks wonderful, doesn't she?' said Mum.

Melissa fell on the bed and rolled around, snorting with laughter.

'Shut up! I hate you!' I said furiously.

'Will you stop that silly sniggering at

once, Melissa. I don't know what's got into you,' said Mum. 'And Martina, I've told you before, you don't *hate* anyone, especially not your sister.'

'Yes, I do!' I mouthed at Melissa, who kept right on spluttering.

'We'll show Dad. I bet you he'll say you look gorgeous,' said Mum.

Dad was actually busy with clients – two elderly ladies who wanted to go on a coach trip. Mum always said we had to leave Dad strictly alone when he was working, but this time she led me straight downstairs and into his office.

'Look at Martina, Harry,' she said, pushing me through the door.

Dad looked. Then he staggered and clapped his hands to his eyes.

'Dad?'

'I'm blinded by your beauty, Marty!'

'Oh, *Dad*!'

'My, what a little princess!' said one of the old ladies.

'Such a beautiful dress! You never see kiddies wearing proper dresses nowadays. Oh, she looks a picture,' said the other one.

'There!' said Mum triumphantly. 'Now come along, Martina, I'll drive you to the dancing school.'

She steered me into the car and we drove off.

'Crash the car, Mum, then I won't have to go,' I muttered.

'Stop it! And don't wind that window down, it'll muck up your hair.'

'But I feel sick. Mum, I think I'm really going to be sick.' I made tentative retching noises.

'Martina Michaels, I have never

smacked you in my life, but if you're deliberately sick all over your beautiful new dress I shall put you over my knee and spank you. Now for goodness' sake, stop acting up. And smooth your skirt, you're getting it creased.'

Mum drove horribly cautiously and carefully, and we arrived at Alisha's dancing school all in one piece. There were cars parked up and down the road, with flocks of girls getting out to go to the party.

I felt real sick churning in my stomach. They were all wearing the sort of clothes Melissa likes: puppy and kitten and bunny T-shirts, sparkly tops with hearts, little tight skirts or long ones with ruffles, pink jeans, white jeans – but no dresses, not a single dress anywhere.

'Mum!' I said, hunching down inside

the car. 'Mum, look at them! I *can't* go to the party, not dressed like this. They'll all wet themselves laughing at me.'

'You're *going* to the party and that's final,' said Mum, practically dragging me out of the car.

I knew I wasn't allowed to hate anyone, but I hated Mum at that moment. And I hated all those girls, who gawked at me as Mum frog-marched me into the dancing hall. I especially hated Katie and Ingrid. Katie was wearing a bright pink halter top and matching jeans, showing lots of bare tummy, and Ingrid was in a sparkly vest thing and a tight skirt. They took one look at me and *rocked* with laughter. I felt my face flushing as violently pink as Katie's outfit.

I was all set to run for it, but Mum held me tight, practically dragging me up to the end of the hall. Mrs Evans was standing next to a bony woman with a topknot, who turned out to be Miss Suzanne, the lady who owned the dancing school. And there was the birthday girl herself!

It was bizarrely comforting to see Alisha prancing around in her lilac dress, because she looked just as ridiculous as me – probably even more so. Her puff sleeves cut into her podgy arms and her skirt stuck up at the front. She was wearing weird white lace tights, so it looked as if she had bandages all over both legs, and she had purple sequin shoes with heels. They were only very little heels, but she wobbled as she walked and her bottom stuck out. Her hair was teased into a grown-up style like a helmet. She was wearing *make-up* too – pink

glossy stuff on her lips and lilac shadow like bruises on her eyelids.

I stared at her. Mum gave me a nudge.

'Happy birthday, Alisha,' I said, and handed her a present.

I knew what it was: a great big tin of felt-tip pens with special fluorescent shades like stinging yellow and sharp lime green and hot orange. I'd have given anything for a set of felt tips like that. I could design any number of outfits for Mighty Mart and have her defeating a herd of yellow hyenas in a green jungle while the orange sun set behind. None of these possibilities occurred to Alisha. She tore off the silver wrapping paper, glanced at the tin, and then put it with a whole pile of presents on a table. She didn't even bother to open it!

'They're special fluorescent felt tips,' I said.

'Thank you,' said Alisha, turning away from me and

starting on Katie's present. It was a stationery set – a little notebook and pen and pencils. I knew for a fact that they were a giveaway on a girls' comic, but Alisha went mad.

'Oh, Katie! They're so lovely! Oh, you're so kind!' she simpered. 'They're the best present *ever*!'

I was about to stomp off into a corner but Miss Suzanne caught hold of me, marvelling at my dress. I was forced to stand there while she pinched my puff sleeves and held up my skirts, practically showing everyone my new knickers.

'What a *beautiful* dress! I thought Alisha's was exquisite, but this is even better!' she whispered to Mum. 'Did *you* go to this magic dressmaker Mrs Evans told me about?'

Mum smiled. '*I'm* the magic dressmaker,'

she said. She gave me a little nod, as if to say, '*See!*'

Miss Suzanne gushed for England while I stood there, agonized.

'Mum, I really really don't feel very well,' I whimpered, tugging at her arm. 'Can't I just go home?'

Miss Suzanne put her arm round me. 'It's all right, dear. Everyone feels a bit shy at parties at first.' She smiled at Mum. 'Don't worry, I'll look after her.'

And she did, oh she did, relentlessly. I had to join in every single one of those old-fashioned party games like Musical Chairs and Blind Man's Bluff. I was nearly last at Musical Chairs, but Ingrid pulled the chair away from me so that Katie got it first. They both poked me hard during Blind Man's Bluff. I endured this, silent and proud, but Miss Suzanne intervened on my behalf.

'Now, now, Ingrid, I think that's cheating. Poor Martina!' she said. And, 'Oh, Katie, I saw that! Don't poke, sweetheart, it hurts!'

It made Katie and Ingrid hate me even more. *They're* allowed to hate all they want. School was going to be a picnic on Monday. Not.

Then we had special dancing games and these were even worse. For Musical Statues we had to pair up and *polka* round the room till the music stopped. I didn't have any proper friends here so there was no one to be my partner. I wondered if I might be paired with Alisha because she didn't have any proper friends either, but she danced with this awful smarmy-looking boy cousin wearing a proper suit with a white shirt and a polka-dot bow tie! He held her in a weird way and stuck his head to one side, and stepped out on tiptoe in his black patent shoes, just like they do in *Strictly Come Dancing*.

I stood against the wall, grateful for

small mercies, when I saw Miss Suzanne advancing towards me.

'Come along, Martina! Come and dance with me!' she said.

'I can't do this dance,' I said quickly.

'Of course you can, dear. It's just step-step-step-*hop*. Anyone can do the polka.'

Anyone but me. I stumbled all over the place as she whirled me round and round the hall at a terrifying pace.

'*You should see me dance the polka!*' she sang in my ear, with great emphasis.

I could see *me* dancing the polka, because there were mirrors all round the hall. It wasn't a pretty sight.

'There, I *think* you're getting the hang of it,' Miss Suzanne said doubtfully.

When she announced the next dance, something called the Gay Gordons, she seized some little sister in a Walt Disney Snow White dress and suggested I dance with her. Snow White was only about four and didn't know the dance either, so we edged into a corner and twirled about doing our own thing.

'You dance funny,' she said.

I didn't think this was a compliment.

Then we were led into the next room, which had trestle tables all pushed together and laid with an incredible birthday tea. When Melissa and I have birthday teas, there are pizza slices and crisps and carrot sticks and cheese-and-pineapple, and then chocolate birthday cake.

This was a grand grown-up tea with tiny sandwiches without crusts, weeny smoked salmon and cream cheese bagels, little scones with jam and cream, and doll-sized cakes laid out in patterns on pretty china plates. Then there were bowls of trifle and tiramisú, and a special ice-cream cake, and a raspberry pavlova, and a cheesecake, and a profiterole tower, *and* an enormous birthday cake with a picture of a ballet dancer in a lilac dress.

I might not be any good at dancing but I am a great eater. I sat next to Snow White and helped her to sandwiches and taught her how to drink her lemonade punch through a straw. I showed her how to blow bubbles too, but I got so enthusiastic,

my bubbles overflowed my glass and a little dribble went down the front of my dress. I scrubbed at it quick with a paper serviette – and saw I'd somehow spilled some ice-cream when I was showing Snow White how to chop it up into little bricks to make a miniature igloo. I scrubbed at that too. There was so much material in my wretched dress that I hoped two weeny little stains wouldn't really be noticed. I was determined not to worry about what Mum would say. I was almost starting to enjoy myself now.

We had to sing 'Happy Birthday' to Alisha, with Mrs Evans and Miss Suzanne conducting us. Then Alisha blew out her candles while her mother sprinkled her with sparkling confetti stuff. She said it was fairy dust and would make all Alisha's dreams come true.

I knew this was silly nonsense, but even so I edged up to Alisha so that some of the fairy dust rubbed off on me. Then I shut my eyes and wished that I could create a proper comic about Mighty Mart. Then she'd be turned into a TV series and a major feature film and a best-selling computer game, and I'd make lots and lots of money, and then Dad wouldn't have to try to be a travel agent any more. He could just go on all these holidays himself, and take me with him. And perhaps Mum too, if she promised not to nag and make me wear stupid dresses. I wasn't sure about Melissa. I remembered how she'd snorted with laughter. Perhaps she'd have to stay home all by herself.

When we'd all had a piece of birthday cake, we had to go back into the main hall and sit on the floor while this clown called Chum-Chum entertained us. Snow White nestled closer to me and whispered that she didn't like clowns, especially ones with white faces and red noses like Chum-Chum. I put my arm round her and said she didn't have to worry, Chum-Chum looked like a nice friendly clown and wasn't a bit scary.

Chum-Chum caught my eye at this point. He took in my elaborately awful dress. 'Ah, you must be the birthday girl!' he said. 'Would you like to come on stage and help me with my magic tricks?'

The *real* birthday girl happened to be in the toilet at that moment. This was too good a chance to miss. I'd always *longed* to do magic tricks.

I leaped up onto the stage. 'I'm happy to be your assistant, Mr Chum-Chum!' I said.

We did a few tame tricks first. I had to keep picking cards and pulling strings of hankies out of his pocket. Then he produced a top hat and my heart started thumping hard. Was he going to pluck a rabbit from the hat? And if so, *would he let me keep it*?

We didn't have any pets at home. Mum wasn't very keen on the idea because she said they made a mess. Could she possibly object to one teeny weeny little rabbit who mostly lived in a hat? I could call my pet rabbit Magic and we could perform tricks together . . .

'Wakey-wakey!' said Chum-Chum. 'I said, tap the top hat with the magic wand, little birthday girl.'

'*She's* not the birthday girl! *I* am!' Alisha shrieked, running into the hall.

Mrs Evans bundled me off the stage. I had to watch *Alisha* pull the rabbit out of the hat – a wonderful *baby* rabbit with the cutest floppy ears. Chum-Chum magicked it away again almost immediately, so she didn't get to keep it either. But she *did* get to do the best thing of all. She lay in a big box (quite a feat as there was an awful lot of Alisha to stuff inside, particularly wearing a dress with

three layers of net petticoat) and she got sawn in half! I *so* wished I could have got sawn in half. It would be so cool. One half of me could stay at home with Dad and draw Mighty Mart comic strips and watch DVDs, and the other half of me could go to school and run around and play football. Alisha looked dead worried though, almost as if she was going to cry. Mrs Evans didn't look happy either. Perhaps she was scared that the precious party dress would be sawn in half too.

I don't think Chum-Chum *really* did it, though his saw certainly looked sharp enough, because Alisha came back on stage all in one piece and her dress wasn't even split across the seams and there was no sign of blood anywhere. Chum-Chum ended his act by *playing* his saw as if it was a musical instrument, and we all sang along to the tunes.

Some of the parents started arriving, so I thought it was time to go home at last

– but Miss Suzanne clapped her hands and announced, 'It's time for the birthday ballet, children!'

My heart started hammering all over again, wondering if I had to attempt *ballet* now – but thank goodness I didn't have to do anything, except be part of the audience.

All the dancing-school pupils rushed backstage to get changed for their big moment. All the girls took part – *and* the smarmy boy cousin. Even little Snow White appeared on the stage and pointed her toes and did a bit of skipping.

The star of the birthday ballet was Alisha, of course. She whirled and twirled around like a very large spinning top, while Mr Evans recorded her grand performance on a camcorder. Katie and Ingrid had to do a little duet. I hoped they'd look incredibly stupid so I could laugh very loudly, but they did modern dancing, wiggling about like girls in a pop group – the sort of dancing Melissa did in front of her mirror, but irritatingly, they were better at it.

The *best* dancer, though, was the boy cousin. He'd changed into the most embarrassing tights instead of trousers, worn with a little tunic that didn't cover enough – but he leaped right up in the air, his legs twiddling this way and that, and then he bent down like a frog and jumped about, and he even turned cartwheels. If *that* was ballet, then maybe I liked it after all.

Mum had arrived by this time. I saw her deep in conversation with Miss Suzanne. I clapped the cousin enthusiastically and I clapped a little bit for Alisha just to be polite, and then I ran up to Mum.

'Are you fixing up for me to have ballet lessons, Mum?' I asked eagerly.

Mum looked amazed.

Miss Suzanne laughed. 'Perhaps dancing isn't quite

your special thing, Martina. You didn't seem to take to the polka very happily.'

'No, I don't mean that silly hoppity-skippety dancing. I want to leap about and do big bunny jumps and cartwheels like him,' I said, pointing to Alisha's cousin.

Miss Suzanne patted me on the head. 'No, darling, *girls* don't do *that* sort of dancing!' she said, and laughed at me again.

'That's not fair! I bet I could do it as good as him,' I muttered, while Miss Suzanne and Mum yacked on about *flower fairies* – rose and poppy and bluebell and soppy sweet-pea fairies. They talked for *ages*, until we were practically the last people left in the hall.

Then, when Mum took me home at last, I got another nasty shock. Dad and Melissa were cuddled up on the sofa dipping oven chips in a saucer of tomato sauce and watching *Toy Story 3* together. That's *my* favourite treat and *my* favourite DVD.

I always watch it with Dad, and we chant along to all the best bits and have to hold hands tight when the toys are about to be rubbished. Maybe *that's* the worst thing about my sister. She's so sneaky, the way she cosies up to Dad the minute my back's turned.

'That's not fair!' I wailed. 'I want to watch too! Can we go back? And can't *I* have any chips?

'Hey, sweetheart, you've been to your party! I felt Melissa needed a little treat too,' said Dad.

'Going to the party wasn't a *treat*, it was total torture,' I said, trying to jam myself in between Melissa and Dad. 'Come on, let's go right back to the beginning.'

'Watch that tomato sauce!' Mum said – a fraction too late.

The saucer jumped up and landed on my blue silk lap.

'Oh, Martina! You've ruined that lovely dress! How could you be so careless!' said Mum.

I thought I was really for it now, but weirdly she didn't seem *ultra*-cross. She whipped the dress off me and tried sponging the sauce off. Then she discovered the lemonade dribble and the ice-cream blob and had another go at me, but only mildly.

'I'm going to get you a great big plastic baby bib and make you wear it every time you eat,' she said. 'Watch the end of *Toy Story 3*, then. You can't possibly start at the beginning, it's nearly bedtime.' She dabbed at the blue dress again.

'Is it really ruined? So I won't ever have to wear it again?' I said hopefully.

'Probably,' said Mum. 'Don't look so pleased!'

'I'm sorry, Mum. I didn't muck it up on purpose.'

'I know.' She sighed. 'You did look lovely in it, Martina. I should have taken a photo of you. Still, it seems to have served its purpose!'

I didn't know what Mum meant – *then*.

We usually all have a family lie-in on Sundays, but Mum was up very early, whirring away on her sewing machine. Dad came sloping into my Marty Den in his pyjamas, scratching his head and yawning.

'Have you got a bunk bed going spare, Marty?' he asked. 'Mum's making a terrible racket in my room.'

'Just chuck Jumper on the floor, Dad. Welcome aboard,' I said.

Dad climbed in, scrunching himself up small. 'Ouch!' he said, feeling under the duvet. 'What's this prickly thing?'

'Oh, that's Percy, my pet porcupine. I wondered where he'd got to,' I said.

'Your porcupine? Of course,' Dad said, tossing my porcupine out into the cold and snuggling down.

I lay down too and thought about the party. I kicked off my duvet and twiddled my legs about, trying to work out how that boy cousin had managed to corkscrew himself up and down.

'What are you *doing*, Marty? The bunk bed's shaking,' said Dad.

'I'm trying to do that boy ballet stuff,' I said. 'Only I can't figure out quite how.'

‘Perhaps it’s easier out of bed,’ Dad suggested.

I jumped down and started leaping around the room. I tried a big twiddle and ended up in a heap on the rug.

‘Oh dear,’ said Dad. ‘Are you all right, Marty?’

I lay still, thinking about it. ‘I’m not sure,’ I said. I kicked my legs tentatively. ‘I think I hurt a bit. My leg.’

‘Which one?’ said Dad, leaning out of the bunk bed and prodding me gently.

‘This one. No, maybe that one. I think they’re both hurting. Perhaps I’ve broken them. Oh, that would be so cool, because then I’ll get plaster. You can have all different colours. Can I have red, Dad?’

‘Yes, and a red nose too, you little clown. I don’t think your legs *are* broken, Curlynob. See if you can get up and walk around a bit.’

‘I helped Mr Chum-Chum at Alisha’s party. He was a clown. I was good at it too.

I nearly got to pull a rabbit out of a top hat,' I said, walking round in circles. 'Dad, could I be a clown when I'm grown up? Girls are allowed to be clowns, aren't they?'

'I don't see why not. I can't say I've *seen* any lady clowns, but I dare say you could be the first.'

'Terrific! I'd better start practising right now. Have you got any saws in your tool box, Dad? I could take it to school and try cutting Katie and Ingrid in half.'

'Well, yes, I *think* girls are allowed to be mass murderers too, but it's not a career path I'd recommend,' said Dad.

'I could just try to play music on your saw, Dad. Mr Chum-Chum made *lovely* music. Go on, let me have a go.'

'Marty, I am generally the most sweet and loving and indulgent dad, you know that – but I'm not letting you muck about with my saw, or any of my other tools. Do you think I'm mad?'

'I think you're an old meanie,' I said. 'What *can* I play, then?'

'I used to play tunes with a piece of toilet paper and a comb,' Dad mumbled.

'Aha!'

I didn't *have* a comb – well, not one with any teeth left – but I remembered that when I'd snaffled Melissa's hairbrush, it had a matching little comb.

I tiptoed out of my den in my pyjamas, took a deep breath, and crept into Melissa's room. Her pink ruffled curtains were still pulled shut. Melissa was lying motionless under her cherry blossom duvet. I padded in bare feet over her deep pink carpet, knelt down on the fluffy rug in front of her dressing table and ever so carefully pulled the top drawer open.

Melissa had her drawer so *organized*: slides sparkling in a straight line, ribbons

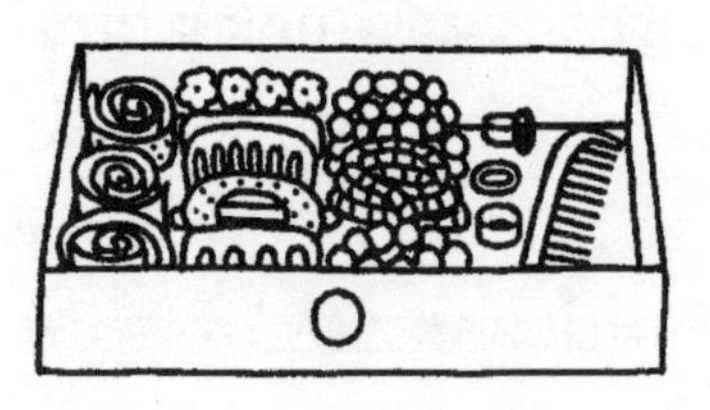

wound into balls, necklaces and bracelets curled up like little snakes – and a pink comb lying there, just begging to be turned into a musical instrument.

I snatched it up.

'What are you *doing*?' said Melissa from under her duvet.

'Nothing!' I said, shoving the comb up my pyjama top.

'Marty!' Melissa sat bolt upright. 'What are you doing in my room? You're not allowed in here.'

'I was just seeing if you were awake, that's all,' I said.

'Well, I am *now*.'

'Sorry. You go straight back to sleep, Melissa – it's Sunday,' I said, and got out of there quick as a wink.

I went into the bathroom and folded some toilet paper over the comb and tried to play it. Then I trailed back to my Marty Den.

'Dad, it doesn't *work*!'

'What? Marty, I'd just dozed off!'

'The toilet paper just turns to pink mush in my mouth – look! Yuck! Why does *everything* have to be pink in this wretched house?'

'Pink mush? Oh! No, it's the wrong *sort* of toilet paper. You need that old-fashioned slippery strong stuff. You know, like Great-Gran has in her toilet.'

I padded off to the cupboard under the stairs to see if we had that kind of paper hidden away, but we only had the soft sort that puppies like to play with. I stared at the washing powder and the kitchen mop and the vacuum cleaner . . . I looked at it long and hard. Our vacuum cleaner is the sort where you slot in all kinds of tubes with different brushes on the end.

I picked up one of the tubes and blew down it tentatively. It made the most

wonderful mournful elephant sound. I blew again, harder. It was incredible! It sounded like a whole herd of elephants now. I blew rhythmically, trying to play 'Happy Birthday'. Then the cupboard door burst open and Mum peered in, looking mad.

'Martina Michaels! Put that down! It's seven o'clock on a Sunday morning. Are you crazy? Are you trying to wake the entire neighbourhood?'

'I'm just trying to play a tune, Mum. Did you hear? I can play "Happy Birthday"!'

'Yes, I *did* hear. So did the whole street. Now come *out* of this cupboard.'

'I think I might be really musical, Mum. Can I have a real musical instrument? Can I have something you blow, like a trumpet? I could have proper music lessons.'

'I thought you were all set on dancing lessons.'

'I don't think I could ever do those twiddly things with my legs.' I emerged from the cupboard under the stairs. 'Look, Mum – what am I doing wrong?' I said, leaping up and trying to get my legs to cross backwards and forwards.

'Quite a lot,' said Mum. 'Come and help me make breakfast seeing as we're all awake now. If you're really serious about dancing, perhaps we *could* start sending you to Miss Suzanne's. I'm sure she'd give us a discount. I'm going to be doing quite a lot of work for her. In fact I need to talk to you and Melissa about something.'

'What?'

'Well, we'll have breakfast first. Shall we have toasted bacon sandwiches?'

'Oh, yes please! Can I fry the bacon, Mum? I love it when it sizzles.'

'You can do the toast – if you're *careful*.'

I loved seeing the toast jump out of the toaster. I got a bit carried away while

Mum was busy frying the bacon. I so liked my toasting job that I kept making more and more, until I'd used up a whole packet of sliced bread.

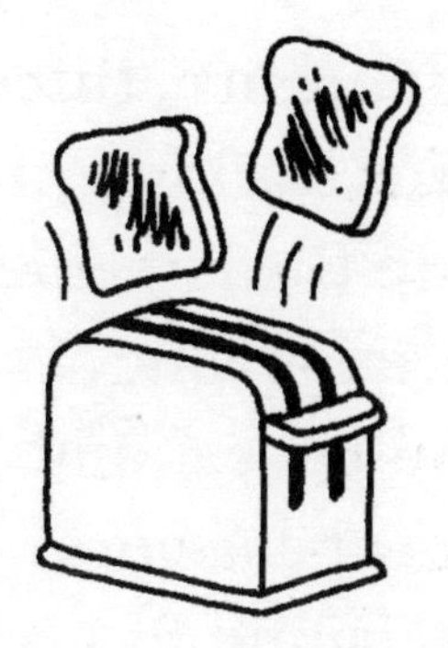

'Martina!' said Mum when she saw.

'It's OK, I'll eat them all – I'm starving,' I said. 'I just love the way they go *pop* out of the toaster.'

'Why can't you ever do anything *sensibly*? Now, get buttering. Eight slices. *Only* eight, all right?'

Mum made the tea and pieced together all the bacon sandwiches.

'Shall I call Dad and Melissa?' I asked.

'We'll have breakfast in bed. Shall we go into your room and sit on your bunk beds?' said Mum.

I hesitated. I didn't really want my Marty Den invaded. I loved having Dad there as a guest, but he didn't nag about tidying my stuff or notice all the underwear lying around in heaps. And I certainly didn't want Melissa going in my room because she always tried to reclaim stuff and boss me about. But the idea of us all eating bacon sandwiches in my bunk beds did sound fun, so I said yes.

Mum and Dad took the bottom bunk, while Melissa and I sat on the top bunk, munching away.

'This is such a weirdo room, Marty,' said Melissa. She stared around at my Mighty Mart posters, and Jumper with his legs in the air, and my plastic horses in their shoe box stable, and Polly, my pretend parrot, crouching on my lampshade, and Basil, my beautiful brown boa constrictor. Luckily my porcupine lurked in the shadows out of sight.

'It's a room with personality,' said Dad loyally.

'Is that what you call it?' said Mum, peering around. Unfortunately she peered upwards too. 'Martina, what on *earth* are those awful black marks on the ceiling?'

Oh dear, they'd happened when I was playing with Baby Monkey, trying to teach him to fly, like those wonderful scary flying monkeys in *The Wizard of Oz*. He'd been *Melissa's* baby monkey. I didn't borrow him – she gave him to me when she was turning out her toy cupboard. Baby Monkey said he didn't want to be pink any more. I quite understood. I got the shoe polish and gave him a thorough massage all over, and he *loved* turning black. He learned to fly very quickly too. He was almost too good at it, and kept hitting the ceiling, leaving one or two little shoe-polish smudges. Still, at least he couldn't get into trouble now, because he'd flown right out of the window and totally disappeared.

'This room's going to need painting all over,' said Mum. She was looking at the carpet. 'And there's that awful stain from when you made such a pig of yourself with your birthday chocolates and then didn't get to the bathroom in time.'

'I was experimenting – seeing how many I could eat in one go. It was a terrific result. I very nearly managed the whole box,' I said.

'I suppose I could cover the stain with a rug, but this room could really do with a new carpet. And we'll have to get rid of that old chair and chest of drawers – they look awful.'

I didn't have proper furniture in my Marty Den. I had a lovely old armchair, probably worth a fortune as a genuine antique. It sagged a bit and there were springs sticking out of one side, but it was still absolutely great for jumping on. My chest of drawers was lovely too, even though it was missing its middle drawer. I'd tried to use it as a sled last winter when it snowed. Somehow it got bashed out of shape and wouldn't ever slot back.

'It's OK, Mum, I *like* my chair and my chest of drawers,' I said.

'No, it's time you slept in a *proper* bedroom, darling,' said Mum.

'Are you going to give Marty's room a whole new makeover?' asked Melissa. 'That's not fair! I want *my* bedroom all done up – it's far too babyish the way it is now.'

'Yes, all right. You can certainly have it redecorated if you like,' said Mum.

Melissa and I stared at each other. Mum doesn't usually give in and say yes to things – well, not straight away.

'Really?' said Melissa quickly. 'Well, thanks, Mum! How fantastic! Can I have a huge new walk-in wardrobe?'

'Don't be silly, that sort of wardrobe would take up far too much room. It's going to be a bit squashed as it is,' said Mum.

'Would someone mind filling me in on all these grandiose plans?' said Dad. 'Especially as I'm the handyman around the house and likely to be the poor chap doing all this painting and decorating and building new wardrobes and the like.' He ruffled Mum's hair as if she were a girl like us. 'What's going on in that funny head of yours, eh? I can feel something whirring away in there. It sounds just like your sewing machine!'

Mum took a deep breath. She leaped off

the bunk bed and faced us. She had bright pink cheeks and her eyes sparkled. She kept clasping and unclasping her hands. That's *my* habit, but I only do it when I want something really, really badly.

'Suzanne from the dancing class has commissioned me to make the costumes for her new children's flower ballet. It's twenty dresses, all with different designs. It's certainly going to be a challenge. But if I do a good job, she thinks she'll be doing a winter pantomime, and that'll mean several changes of costume for each child. And two of the mothers at the party have asked if I'd make their daughters' bridesmaids' dresses. One of them wants *six* bridesmaids' dresses plus a little flower-girl outfit. I'll be sewing day and night, but it'll be worth it. You should hear what they're paying me!'

'That's wonderful, Jan,' said Dad.

'Fantastic, Mum,' said Melissa.

'All those lovely dresses! I'm so glad *I* won't ever have to wear one again,' I said.

'Was it all down to me being a good advert for your sewing skills, Mum?'

'I think it must have been,' she said. 'Thank you for being an excellent child model, Martina.'

I laughed and bowed to her from my top bunk.

'So we're getting our bedrooms decorated because you're going to make lots of money?' asked Melissa.

'Well, the thing is . . . I've been trying to figure out how to manage all this extra work. It's going to be so awkward if I have people trooping in and out of my bedroom to get measured and try clothes on. It doesn't look professional, with the bed right in the middle of the room – especially if it's not made properly.'

'Sorry, sorry,' said Dad, holding his hands in the air.

'And then I'm going to need a lot of

space to *hang* the dresses. Ideally I should hang them all around the room, protected by polythene.' Mum gestured, pointing all around *my* room – and my heart turned over.

'You can't put all those dresses in my Marty Den, Mum, you simply can't!' I said. 'It wouldn't be sensible! You know how messy I am! I wouldn't *mean* to, but I'd get those dresses mucked up in no time.'

'I know you would, love,' said Mum. 'But perhaps if we *moved* you . . . ? You see, I really *need* this room as a sewing room.'

I was so astounded I could barely speak. I felt as if Mum had punched me hard, right in the stomach. 'You want to push me out of my very own Marty Den?' I whispered.

I hardly ever cry – it's such a stupid girlie thing to do – but somehow I had tears running down my face.

'Oh, Martina, don't cry!' said Mum. She ran up my bunk-bed ladder and sat beside me, hugging me.

'I can't help it. You can't take my Marty Den away, Mum! I haven't even done anything wrong. Well, nothing worse than usual,' I sobbed.

'I know, darling. It's not a punishment. I'm just trying to be practical. And this is such a scruffy old room. We've never really got round to furnishing it properly. I really do need it as a sewing room. But there's no need to be so upset. I'm sure Dad will make you some new shelves if you ask nicely. You can't really like this old stuff, Martina. Your den just looks like a junk room. And girls don't really *have* dens anyway – it's a boy thing.'

'*I* want a den,' I wept.

'So is Marty moving in with you and Dad?' asked Melissa.

Mum swallowed again. 'No, Melissa. I don't think that would work at all,' she said. 'Children don't sleep in their parents' room – not at this age, anyway.'

'Then where is she going to move *to*?' Melissa said. Her voice was rising steadily.

'Well, it's obvious, darling. She'll move in with you,' said Mum.

'No! No, absolutely *not*!' Melissa shrieked. 'I *can't* share with Marty! She'll make a terrible mess and ruin all my things and drive me absolutely mad!'

'Don't worry, I'm not sharing with you ever ever ever!' I declared. 'If Mum takes my Marty Den away, I'll – I'll sleep in the kitchen, under the table – or in the bath – or I'll camp in a tent in the garden!'

'You're both making a silly fuss! Look, it'll be fun for you to share. *I* shared a room with my sister and we loved it. We had all sorts of fun and good times together,' said Mum.

'Yes, but you and Auntie Carol *like* each other,' said Melissa.

'I want you two silly girls to get to like each other too. I know you love each other to bits *really*, but I'm sick and tired of you arguing all the time. Look at you the other day – fighting!'

'But, Mum, we'll be fighting all the time if I have to sleep in that awful pink room – and it *smells* so,' I wailed.

'It does *not* smell!' Melissa retorted.

'Yes it does – of all that yucky rose stuff and powder and hairspray. I shall be as— as— as*phyxiated* if I have to stay in Melissa's room.'

'Well, *I* shall be asphyxiated by the awful pong of your grubby clothes and your stupid ratty old home-made toys. Mum, you *can't* make us share, you simply *can't*!' Melissa said, and she started crying too.

'*Please* don't cry, both of you! Look, I'm sorry, I don't want to upset you. If you'll just see reason, you'll get to *like* the idea, I'm sure you will. You can re-design your room. You *said* you wanted it redecorated, Melissa. Well, now's your chance.'

'But there's no point if Marty's going to be in it. She'll spoil everything! She'll be messing with all my stuff, breaking it, just utterly tormenting me. How can you *do* this to me, Mum?'

'I'm simply trying to do some work and get some extra money for all of us,' said Mum. She looked as if *she* were going to cry too.

'Stop it, all of you,' said Dad. He said it very quietly, but there was something about his voice that made us all shut up. 'There's no need for you to get into such a silly state. Marty, you can keep your den. Melissa, you don't have to share your bedroom. Jan, you can have a special sewing room. You can have the front room downstairs. It's obvious I'm not making enough money in the travel business now. I shall shut up shop altogether. It's been a total failure. Like me.'

Then Dad lay down on the bottom bunk bed and turned his face to the wall.

That shut us up. Melissa and I stopped squabbling. Mum squeezed into the bottom bunk beside Dad and laid her head on his.

'You're not a failure. You're the best husband and father in the world. You've tried so hard, darling. I'm sure the business will pick up soon. Maybe we should start advertising, so that people know you're here. But you *must* keep going. I wouldn't dream of using your room. Look, if the girls are truly desperately unhappy about sharing, then I'll just have to keep on using our bedroom.'

Melissa looked at me. I looked at her. We hunched up close together. We hardly dared look, but it sounded as if Dad was crying.

We were very used to seeing each other in tears. We didn't like it the rare times Mum cried, but it wasn't terrible. But *Dad* crying was the worst thing ever.

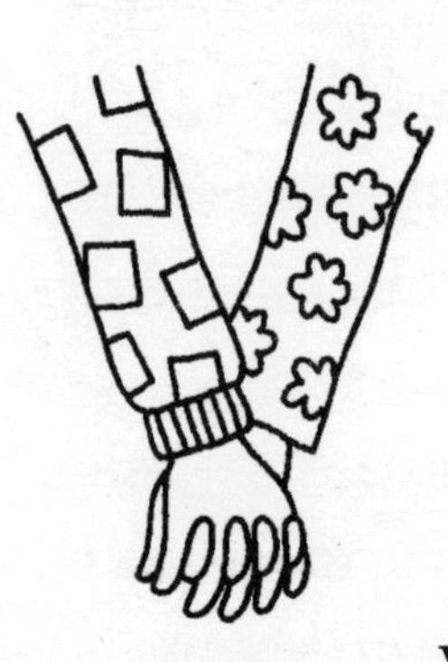

I found myself reaching out for Melissa's hand. She hung onto me, squeezing my hand hard.

'Shall we pretend we don't really mind sharing?' I whispered. 'Even though we *do*.'

'I suppose so,' Melissa whispered back.

I glanced around my wonderful Marty Den, gazing at all my special things. But the most special thing of all was my dad, and I couldn't stand him being upset.

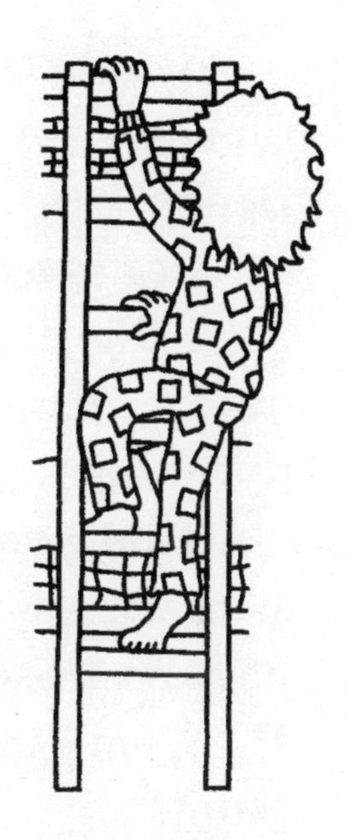

'Hey, change of plan,' I said, swinging down the ladder to the bottom bunk. 'Maybe Melissa and I *will* share.'

'Yes, perhaps it will be fun,' said Melissa bravely. 'So can we really give my room a makeover?'

'Certainly, darling,' said Mum. 'Oh, girls, are you really sure?'

Of course we weren't sure, and everyone knew it – but we were stuck now.

'It'll be great,' I said. 'Though do we have to keep it *pink*? It's the worse colour in the entire rainbow universe.'

'I *like* pink. It's my all-time favourite colour. But maybe my soft *pale* pink is a bit babyish now. Perhaps we could go for a brighter pink. Lipstick pink? Shocking pink? Neon pink! Wouldn't you like neon, Marty?' said Melissa.

'Yes, but it's the pink bit I object to. Couldn't we have red, like in my Marty Den?'

'Red is a crazy colour for a bedroom.'

'I like it. Or maybe purple. We could have two red walls and two purple walls – that would look cool,' I said.

'That would look totally ridiculous,' said Melissa. 'You're hopeless, Marty. You have no sense of colour or style whatsoever. My room's staying pink – isn't that right, Mum?'

'Yes, love, I think it will have to stay pink.'

'That's not fair! You always take Melissa's side,' I wailed.

'She just had her pink carpet last year. We can't afford any major changes. But I think we could certainly add a few bright pink touches, just to jazz it up a bit.' Mum paused. 'Make it like a teenage room.'

'Oh yes!'

'Oh no! It's going to be my room too so

I get to choose just as much as you. Don't I, Dad?'

Dad mumbled something. He still had his head in the pillow, but he had stopped crying now.

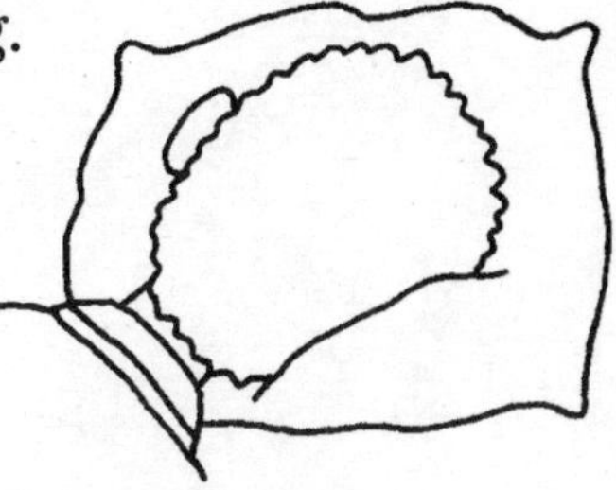

'We'll get one or two magazines, see if they have any features on girls' bedrooms,' said Mum.

'We don't need silly old magazines. Look, I'll draw it for us,' I said.

I searched for my drawing pad. I still couldn't find any proper pens. I shook my school bag out to see if there was one hiding in a crack somewhere. I forgot about my inky PE kit. (I'd had to do two PE lessons in my school blouse and knickers.) The ink had dried so they weren't soggy any more – but they were remarkably *black*. I tried to stuff them straight back in my bag, but Mum saw, even though she was still cosied up to poor Dad.

'For goodness' sake, Martina, what's

that on the floor? It's not . . . it can't be your PE kit!'

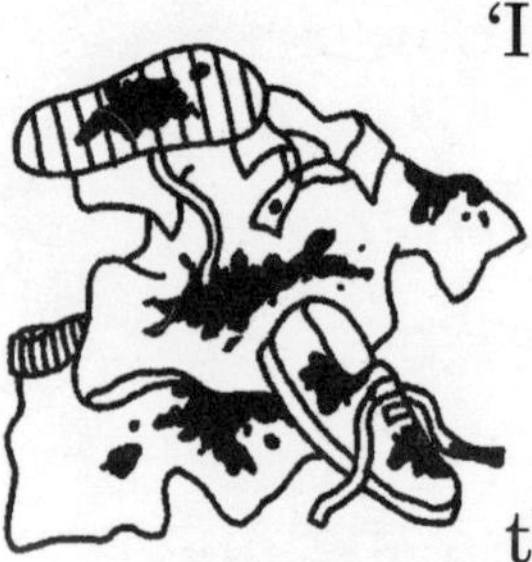

'I think it needs a bit of a wash, Mum,' I said. 'Oh bother, I still haven't got any decent pens. I borrowed Jaydene's yesterday but I can't find that either.'

'What's the *matter* with you, Martina? I bought you a pack of *five* uniballs just last month. And just look at the state of your PE kit! How am I ever going to get that clean? It's *black*.'

'What about a touch of black for my room, Mum? It would look dead sophisticated,' said Melissa. 'A black furry rug, say? I know! I could have a black chandelier-type thing – that would look *so* cool.'

'What's a chandelier?' I asked suspiciously.

'It's a kind of light. Look – find a pen and I'll draw it for you,' said Melissa.

'I'll get you both a pen. I'm sure I've got

some downstairs,' said Dad. His voice still sounded a bit funny. He wriggled out of bed, his head bent, and shuffled downstairs in his pyjamas. All three of us were silent for a second, staring after him worriedly.

'Do you think he's all right now?' I whispered.

'Poor old dad,' said Melissa, sighing.

'I feel really bad,' Mum said softly. 'I didn't mean to make him unhappy. I just got so carried away because I've got orders for all these dresses. Oh, girls, you're so sweet to say yes to sharing. It'll work out, you'll see.'

'Yes, we'll get along just fine,' said Melissa. 'As long as Marty doesn't mess with all my things and drive me mad.'

'We'll manage, Mum,' I said. 'As long as Melissa doesn't boss me about and tell me what to do all the time.'

Dad was a while coming back. We heard him go into the bathroom first. When he came back to the Marty Den at last, he'd washed his face and brushed his hair so you couldn't tell he'd been crying at all. He brought us a pen each and kept one for himself, and got up on the top bunk between us.

'Now, let's sketch out this gorgeous new bedroom,' he said. 'I think you'll maybe need some new shelves and storage space.'

'Oh *yes*, Dad!' said Melissa.

'Well, you two be the designers, and I'll see what I can do,' said Dad. 'You'll help me paint them, won't you, Marty?'

'You bet, Dad,' I said.

I nestled close and he put his arm round me. He was acting as if everything was absolutely fine now. I smiled at him and he smiled right back at me, but his eyes still looked unhappy.

I felt unhappy too, because I hated the idea of losing my lovely cosy private Marty Den. But Melissa was getting carried away now, designing a new bedroom, and Mum was over the moon, singing away happily when she went back to her sewing.

I tried to get involved with the design of this pale-pink and neon-pink and black room, but Melissa was so *bossy*. I drew my chair in my plan, and she scribbled all over it. Maybe *that's* the worst thing about my sister – she's so domineering.

'We're *not* having that awful old chair,' Melissa said. 'We'll have *new* chairs.'

'Hey, hey, I don't think we can afford new furniture, girls,' said Dad.

'Well, I'd sooner go without than have

that awful heap of junk cluttering up the place. *I* know, Mum could get some black velvet material down the market and we could make huge great squashy cushions and sit on them,' said Melissa.

'Excellent idea!' said Dad.

I wanted to come up with an excellent idea, but I didn't know much about boring old bedrooms. I drew Mighty Mart in her den instead. She lived in a loft all by herself, and she had a huge bed that she shared with all her cats and dogs. They had superpowers too. They could all talk, and the cats could fly and the dogs could all run faster than tigers, even the weeny Chihuahua. Mighty Mart didn't bother with boring stuff like wardrobes because she wore the same blue tunic and red tights and orange cape all the time, and she *certainly* didn't wear make-up or bother with her hair, so she didn't need a dressing table.

I drew her a trampoline to fill up some

of the white space, but then I had to make a neat hole in the ceiling to stop her bumping her head.

'Could we have a teeny tiny trampoline in the middle of our new room?' I asked.

'Oh, Marty, don't be *stupid*! A trampoline! You don't have trampolines in *bedrooms*,' said Melissa scornfully.

'I don't see why not. I think it would be super cool. *Could* we have a trampoline, Dad?'

'I don't think the floorboards would stand it, Marty,' he said. 'We'll see about a trampoline for the garden – when we've got a bit more money to spare.'

I drew Mighty Mart a trapeze too, which she absolutely loved. She learned to do the most amazing tricks because she could fly already, so she wasn't afraid of falling.

'Could we have a trapeze in our new room?' I asked.

'You are *so* stupid, Marty. I think you're just doing it on purpose! A *trapeze*!'

'They're indoor things, trapezes. And it wouldn't take up much room. You could just fix it to the ceiling, couldn't you, Dad? And I could do all sorts of tricks on it, couldn't I?'

'Do you remember what happened when you did all sorts of tricks on the swings in the park?' Dad said gently.

I fingered the bumpy bit on my head where I'd had stitches.

'It's not fair if I can't have *anything* I want in this new bedroom,' I said.

'Yes, but you just want stupid things,' said Melissa, happily colouring with *my* pink felt tip.

'Do you mind? That's *my* pink felt tip, and I particularly need to keep the colour because Mighty Mart sometimes flies way up into the stratosphere to this scary pink planet to sort out all these pink alien weirdos,' I said.

Melissa rolled her eyes. '*You're* the total alien weirdo, Marty. I shall be seriously spooked sharing a room with you. I'm sure one day I'll wake up and see you've turned green with little blobby antennae growing out of your forehead,' she said, still colouring.

She got to the bed shape blocked out in her design. 'What colour duvet covers shall I have? Two shades of pink – or bright pink and black?'

'I'm going to have Wilma Whale, and she's purple and turquoise,' I said.

'*What*? You're not having that awful old thing in my bedroom!'

'It's *our* bedroom – and don't call her awful and old, you'll hurt her feelings,' I said, picking Wilma up and wrapping her around me.

'It's my *bed*. And I don't know what

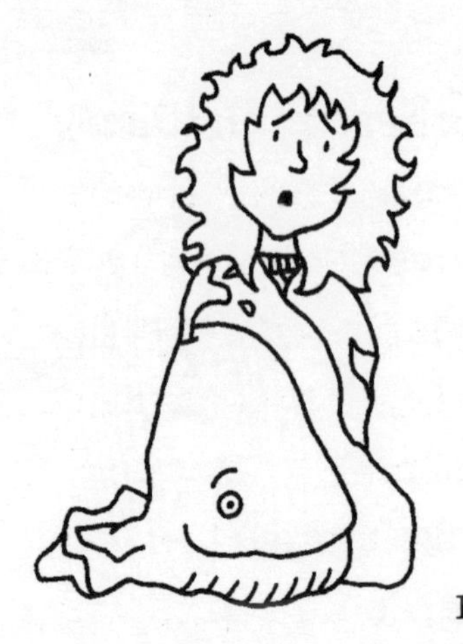

I'm going to do because I don't want *you* in it, with all your manky pretend animals. It's not big enough anyway. You'll have to have your own bed, matching mine,' said Melissa.

'I've got my bunk beds, stupid,' I said.

'You're not having bunk beds in my room! They're way too babyish. It's only little kids who have bunk beds. They'll spoil the whole look of the room.'

'Stop squabbling, you two,' said Dad, busy sketching out his shelf unit. 'I told you, we can't afford new furniture.'

'Can't you *make* us a new bed, Dad?' said Melissa.

'I'm a versatile chap – but I don't think I could,' said Dad. 'I'm going to have my work cut out as it is. I reckon we could have one whole wall for shelves and storage. That should give both of you lots of space.'

But when we measured it out later that morning, we found that there wasn't enough space for Melissa's bed *and* my bunk beds. Well, they *would* just about fit, but they'd be squashed in side by side and we'd have to edge round them.

'It wouldn't make sense to have the bed *and* the bunk beds anyway,' said Mum. 'It's obvious what we're going to have to do. We'll dismantle Melissa's bed and store it somewhere and just keep the bunk beds in the room.'

'Hurray!' I said.

'No, that's an *awful* idea. I hate bunk beds. It will ruin the entire *concept* of my room! I can't cope with this!' Melissa declared, flinging herself about and wringing her hands. Maybe *that's* the worst thing about my sister: she's such a drama queen.

'Oh my, the world's coming to an end! Oh dear, I can't cope!' I mocked, imitating her.

'Shut up, you! Oh, Mum, please, this is

the worst idea in the world. It will never ever work!' said Melissa.

She felt free to make a fuss because Dad had gone off to B&Q to get some sugar soap cleaning stuff to scrub down my Marty Den walls before he started painting.

'Now stop it,' said Mum. 'You two girls have made a decision. Let's stick to it. I'm not having you arguing on and on like this, especially when it's in front of your father. You saw how upset he got.'

'Well, I don't want to upset him, but it's daft, him having the whole room downstairs for his travel agency when no one comes any more,' said Melissa, sticking her chin out. 'Why doesn't he give it up and do something *else*? He's so useless.'

'How dare you! He has tried, you nasty selfish girl,' said Mum. 'We haven't always told you girls, but he's applied for umpteen other jobs in shops and offices, but either they want someone younger or he hasn't got the right qualifications. He's doing his level best. It's not his fault there's a recession. He's worrying himself sick. We're seriously short of money, Melissa. Now that I've got a chance to make some extra cash for the family, we might just start clearing our debts – but it's no use demanding this and that. We can afford a tin or two of paint, some material, a few planks of wood. That's about it. Do you understand?'

Melissa nodded, squirming. I usually liked it the rare times she got the telling-off and not me, but I felt dreadful too. I hated it that poor Dad had tried so hard and got nowhere. I especially hated Melissa for calling him useless.

'Dad isn't useless,' I said. 'He's the best dad ever.'

'I know,' said Melissa. 'Don't tell him I said that, will you? I didn't really mean it.'

'I know you didn't,' said Mum. 'You were

just fed up. We're *all* fed up because we all want to get our own way. Well, I'm sorry, but we've all got to learn to compromise.'

'If you don't mind me saying, Mum, that's a little bit annoying because *you're* not having to compromise. You don't have to lose your special room. You're *gaining* one,' I said.

'My life is one *big* compromise. I have to cook and wash and clean and tidy for all you lot. I have to go out to work at the school, where all the parents ring me up making a fuss. When I eventually get to sew, I'm tired out and I've got a splitting headache. And it's made worse by two spoiled daughters giving me grief!'

It was my turn to squirm now. I mumbled that I was sorry – though I can't say I really meant it. Mum went off to do some more sewing. Melissa went back to her bedroom to start a big clear-out.

I stayed in my Marty Den. I hunched up between Wilma and Jumper with my sketchbook. I looked at Melissa's design. This new bedroom might be for both of us, but it didn't *look* like mine at all.

I drew my bunk beds with a large wing on either side. I sketched myself standing on the top bunk, navigating, as we rose up up up in the air, with Mighty Mart flying along beside us for company.

I was worried about Dad, but now that he had two rooms to work on he perked up a lot. He'd always loved do-it-yourself. Now I was bigger it was do-it-yourself-with-Marty's-help, and *I* loved that.

I came running home from school every day and put on my oldest jeans and my least favourite pink puppy T-shirt, an ancient Melissa cast-off. The puppy soon got so covered in white paint you could only see a pink paw here, a pink ear there.

We tackled Mum's sewing room first.

It was weird seeing my Marty Den start to disappear. I cried a bit when the chair and the chest of drawers were crammed into the back of the car and taken to the tip. I hated having to unstick all my Mighty Mart posters and roll them up. But it was *great* fun doing the painting. Dad did the ceiling and the fiddly bits, but he let me slosh the roller around and do lots of the walls.

I wanted to draw on them first. I so wanted to do a great big portrait of Mighty Mart so she would be there for ever under the paint, but Dad wouldn't let me. He said you must never ever draw on walls. Mighty Mart would start showing through the white paint. I *wanted* her to show through a little, like a ghost. This was her birthplace, after all. Still, I didn't want to make a fuss in case Dad got upset again.

When the paint was dry, he fixed a rail round all four walls so that Mum could hang up her finished costumes. She couldn't afford new carpet so she had to clean mine. She had to do it over and over again, and even then not *all* the stains came out, but she pulled her sewing machine table over the worst patch. She stood her big bedroom mirror in one corner and Little No-Head in the other. This was her old dressmaker's dummy. I had christened her when I was little. I used to play with her, but it's hard work giving a headless person any personality.

Mum's sewing room was ready in three days. We had a little opening ceremony with a bottle of Cava that was on offer in Sainsbury's. I was allowed one sip and Melissa two. I liked the bubbles but didn't go much on the taste.

Then we got started on Melissa's bedroom. Did you note that I said I cried just a tiny bit when my Marty Den was dismantled and my wonderful furniture thrown away? Well, my sister Melissa is two and a half years older than me, but she cried *buckets* when Dad took her silly old bed to bits. It wasn't even getting chucked out, just stowed at the back of the garage. Excuse me – *more* than buckets. Melissa cried gallons and gallons and gallons. She could have filled an entire swimming pool with her tears. She went on and on. 'Oh my poor bed! . . . I know I'll never sleep properly again! . . . Oh, *why* do I have to have Marty's horrible bunk beds cluttering up my room?' Maybe *that's* the worst thing about my sister: she's a terrible crybaby.

It's so unfair, because Mum and Dad sat her down and gave her lots of cuddles and told her she was being very *brave*!

'I just don't get it! Why is Melissa being *brave*? In case you've forgotten, I've lost my entire room, not just a silly old bed!' I said indignantly.

'I know, Martina, but Melissa cares terribly about the way things look. She so set her heart on this bedroom looking perfect,' said Mum. 'I can understand.'

'Well, *I* can't. Dad, don't you think Melissa's making a huge great fuss? *I* didn't cry, did I? Well, hardly at all,' I said.

'I know, Curlynob, you've been very brave too – but you don't care quite so much about the way things look.'

'Yes, I do! I care *passionately*!'

'Martina, you were quite happy living in a positive junk heap, with furniture falling to bits and no clear colour scheme at all,' said Mum.

'But it was just the way I wanted it! It was my Marty Den – and I miss it so,' I said.

I suddenly realized how *much* I was missing my lovely cosy, comfy, den, where I could hunch up with all my favourite animals and draw Mighty Mart in peace. I burst into tears. I couldn't help it. I was *overcome with grief*, honestly, but they wouldn't believe me.

'Stop that silly noise, Martina. You're just doing it to get attention because we're making a fuss of Melissa,' said Mum.

'Come on, little Curlynob, turn off the waterworks,' said Dad.

I wanted to slope off and lurk under my bunk beds, but I couldn't, because they were in Melissa's room now, and there was horrible pink fluffy carpet in my lovely dark hidey-hole, and a dreadful sickly smell of roses everywhere.

'I don't have a *home* any more,' I wailed. 'And neither do Wilma and Jumper and Basil and Polly and Patches and Gee-Up and Sugarlump and Merrylegs and Dandelion and Starlight and Percy.'

'Stop being such a baby, Martina. You're getting too old for all these silly toys,' said Mum.

'Who's Percy?' said Dad.

'My porcupine,' I sobbed. 'And he's starving to death because there are no ants in this room. And what about *Mighty Mart*?'

'She's safe in your head, you noodle,' said Dad. 'Why don't you get out your sketchbook and draw her for a bit to calm yourself down?'

'Yes, that's another thing. Where am I going to put my Mighty Mart posters?' I said, looking around wildly.

'You're not putting those silly scribbly posters on my pink wallpaper!' Melissa shouted.

'Yes, I am so!'

'No, Martina, you ruined your own walls with Sellotape and Blu Tack. I'm not having this room messed up too,' said Mum.

'It's not fair! You always take Melissa's side on everything! I don't know why you bothered to have a second daughter. You love her twice as much as you love me.'

'Hey, hey, calm down, Marty! That's silly talk. You know we love you both the same. Look, I know you're upset about your animals and posters – and I'm going to fix things for you, I promise. I started on the shelf unit today. I'm building it in the garage. I'm making a special cupboard for both of you, as well as lots of shelves – and you can have a cork board at either end so you can both pin up posters or photos – whatever.'

'There won't be enough space for *all* my Mighty Mart posters,' I mumbled. 'And my animals don't want to live in a cupboard. It's cruel to cage them up. They want to roam free.'

I couldn't roam free in Melissa's room. I felt as if I were suffocating. I stayed marooned on my bunk bed with all my animals and drawing stuff while Melissa and Mum kept on making the room worse and worse.

Mum got some silky black material patterned with bright pink peonies and made them into duvet covers and pillow cases for my precious bunk beds. I hadn't much liked my red-and-white bedclothes, but at least they *felt* right. These new ones were all slippery and slidy and gave me the shivers.

Mum bought all this new stuff for Melissa too, even though we were supposed to be so poor now. She bought a furry black rug and a bright pink stool to go with Melissa's dressing table. She even bought her a black chandelier! It was only a little one, with just a few dangling twinkly bits, but I bet it still cost a lot.

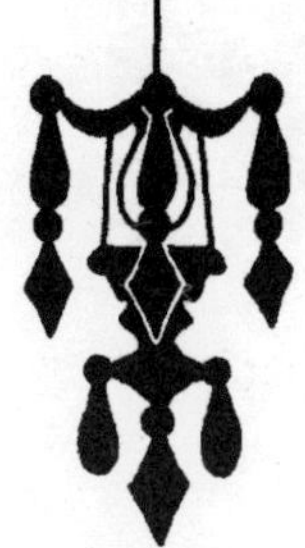

'Oh, Mum, it's magic!' said Melissa.

I stared up at the black chandelier and wished it really *was* magic. Maybe it would start spinning and make everything come right. I would be back in my beloved Marty Den. Melissa could have her wretched pink bedroom to herself. Dad would suddenly get a wonderful new job so that Mum could sew downstairs. All my animals would become real all the time. And I would turn into Mighty Mart and go striding off to school and zap Katie and Ingrid so they'd both turn into ugly little warty toads – and if they didn't watch out, I'd stamp on them.

Katie and Ingrid were giving me serious grief. They had a new nickname for me: *Bluebottle*. This was because of the blue dress I'd worn at Alisha's party. They called it after me at every opportunity.

It wasn't the slightest bit *funny* or *witty* or *original*, but they always howled with laughter when they said it. I made out I didn't care, though I did really. Dreadfully. And then horrible Alisha started calling me Bluebottle too, because she always sucks up to Katie and Ingrid. I almost expected *her* to do that, but I was taken aback when half the class caught on and called me Bluebottle too. Most of them didn't even know *why*, because they hadn't been to Alisha's awful party.

'Never mind, Marty,' said Jaydene,

putting her arm round me. 'Just try to ignore them.'

She was now my very special best friend for ever, and deeply loyal to me, but she wasn't much use at defending me against Katie and Ingrid. Jaydene was very tall and very big, so you'd think she would be a really fierce, fighty girl – but she was a total wuss. She cried if anyone so much as shouted at her. Jaydene was scared of so many things: worms, stepping on the cracks in the pavement, dogs that barked, lifts, swimming, spiders, her strict auntie, maths lessons, stinging nettles . . . I could fill the whole *page*. She was especially scared of Katie and Ingrid.

I had to fight my own battles with them. I wasn't really too fussed about Ingrid. When Katie was off school with chicken pox, Ingrid was almost *nice*. She didn't pick on anyone, or call them names, or sniff and say they smelled disgusting. She played rounders with a whole crowd of us in the playground at lunch time, and when I scored a rounder, she patted me on the back and said I was brilliant. But as soon as Katie came back to school Ingrid changed back to being mean. Even *meaner*. The next time we were playing rounders together, Ingrid pushed me hard as I ran past, and I fell over and was caught out. Everyone *saw*, but no one dared say anything.

Katie didn't ever push anyone, but somehow she was the scariest. She didn't *look* scary. She was little, with a pretty face and long shiny black hair – but inside her little rosebud mouth was a tongue as sharp as a Stanley knife.

I decided I had to sharpen *my* tongue. I brooded on the Bluebottle name-calling. I wasn't quite sure what a bluebottle *was*, so I went to the library at lunch time. It was good to have somewhere to go. I couldn't hang out with Jaydene because she didn't stay for school dinners. She went home for lunch, the lucky thing. I didn't feel like playing rounders or footie or tag, not with people calling me the dreaded B-word.

Mrs Grinstead was on library duty. I *loved* Mrs Grinstead. She was a big, soft, smiley lady with very blue eyes behind her glasses. She wasn't a class teacher, she looked after children with special needs. I always thought how lovely it would be to cosy up to Mrs Grinstead and look at storybooks together and do lots of wax crayoning, instead of having to sit up straight in class and do difficult sums and get poked in the back by Katie and Ingrid.

'Hello, Marty,' said Mrs Grinstead, smiling.

That was another magical thing about her. She knew all our names, even if she didn't teach us.

'What are you looking for today? I've

seen a brilliant new book about polar bears and penguins – and there's a lovely old comic book on the shelf over there.'

Mrs Grinstead is spot-on when it comes to sussing out *exactly* the sort of book I like.

'I think I'd like both, Mrs Grinstead – but actually I'm really here to look something up in a dictionary,' I said.

'Really, Marty? How splendid! Well, we have a very fine selection over here, though they might be a bit dusty. No one ever seems to look at a dictionary nowadays. Here we are, dear.'

She sat me down at a little table and gave me the biggest dictionary of all – so big I could barely lift it. I started flipping through all the B pages. I got side tracked a little, finding all sorts of unexpected words there – even *rude* ones. But then I found *blue-*

bottle, with the definition: *Another name for the blowfly*. So then I had to swap pages and peer all down the list for blowfly, and there it was: *Any of the various dipterous flies of the genus* Calliphora *and related genera that lay their eggs in rotting meat, dung, carrion and open wounds*.

So that told me. I didn't have a clue what at least five of those words meant, but I didn't want to spend the entire lunch time flipping through the dictionary, so I wrote it down. I had to borrow Mrs Grinstead's pen, but I used it very carefully, not pressing too hard, and gave it right back to her. Then I asked her to show me the books she'd mentioned. They were ace, and she let me borrow them both.

I holed up in a corner of the corridor, not wanting to encounter Katie and Ingrid just yet. I needed to come prepared. I read about polar bears and penguins, and then I looked at this brilliant comic book about a boy called Little Nemo. I planned a new

Mighty Mart adventure in the frozen north. She could be queen of a whole tribe of polar bears, and keep a comical gang of penguins as special swimming pets. I usually did Mighty Mart's adventures in little square boxes, but the Little Nemo comic had shown me a different way of doing it.

I intended to creep into the classroom and snaffle a piece of paper and someone's pen to sketch it out, but Mum – of all people – came hurrying along the corridor, dragging along some little kid from the Infants who had been sick all down themselves. Mum didn't look very pleased about it, and she looked even less thrilled to see me.

'Really, Martina, what are you doing skulking indoors? You know perfectly well you're not allowed in the classrooms at lunch time,' she said.

'I'm sorry, Mum – I was just in the library and—'

'I'm sorry, *Mrs Michaels*,' said Mum. She has this daft rule that we have to call her that at school. 'Now off you go straight away.'

'I don't suppose you've got a spare pen on you, Mum— Mrs Michaels?' I asked.

'Please, miss, I think I'm going to be sick *again*!' said the Infant.

'Oh, Lord! Come to the toilets, quick! Martina, go *outside*,' said Mum.

I had to wait till I got home to start on my amazing new Mighty Mart adventure. Jaydene had lent me another of her pens, so I could get cracking straight away. I did the pictures all different sizes, with my characters sometimes sticking an arm or a leg or a paw or a beak out of the main frame. I did an *enormous* king polar bear, as

tall as the whole page, and then a very long, narrow horizontal frame of lots of little penguins waddling across the snow, and then on the next page I had Mighty Mart sliding down an enormous glacier from the top left-hand corner all the way to the bottom right.

I went running out to the garage to show Dad. He was busy putting together all the pieces of our new shelf unit and cupboard space.

'Hey, Marty,' he said, but he didn't even look up.

'Hey, Dad, take a look at my new Mighty Mart adventure!'

'I'd love to see it, Curlynob, but not just now. I'm a bit busy.'

'Oh, Dad, let me show you. I've got ever so good at drawing polar bears – *and* the cutest little penguins – look!'

'Yes, yes, I'd love to see them, but the thing is, I'm trying to sort out your shelving, and it's like a giant jigsaw piece and I'm a bit stuck at the moment.'

'Don't worry, Dad, I'll help you,' I said, bending down and picking up several planks of wood.

'Don't move them! Oh no, I'd just got that bit worked out!'

'Sorry!'

'Push off just now, Marty, there's a love,' said Dad.

So I did. I went to find Mum instead, but she was in her brand-new sewing room with Melissa. Mum was whirring away on her sewing machine, making a poppy dress. It had lots of bright red petals for a skirt, and a black velvet bodice. Melissa was sitting cross-legged

on the floor sewing a big black blobby velvet shape.

'What's that, Melissa?'

'It's a squashy cushion for our room,' she said proudly.

'Oh,' I said, losing interest immediately. 'Look at my new Mighty Mart adventure!'

'No thanks,' said Melissa. 'You and your silly old Mighty Mart comics. They're all the same. She's just a great big you swooping here and there, going *zap-zap-zap*.'

'They are *not* all the same. Especially not my new one. She's having a North Pole adventure, and there are polar bears and penguins – look! I bet you can't draw polar bears and penguins.'

'Like, would I want to?' said Melissa, stitching away.

'You look, Mum,' I said.

'In a minute, dear. I've just got to get this bodice joined on and it's at a very tricky stage,' said Mum.

I sighed hugely and stomped off into my

room. Only it wasn't my room at all, it was Melissa's pink room with my bunk beds squashed into a corner, and all my stuff in cardboard boxes until the shelf unit was finished. I'd insisted on putting all my pets with their heads sticking out so that they could breathe properly.

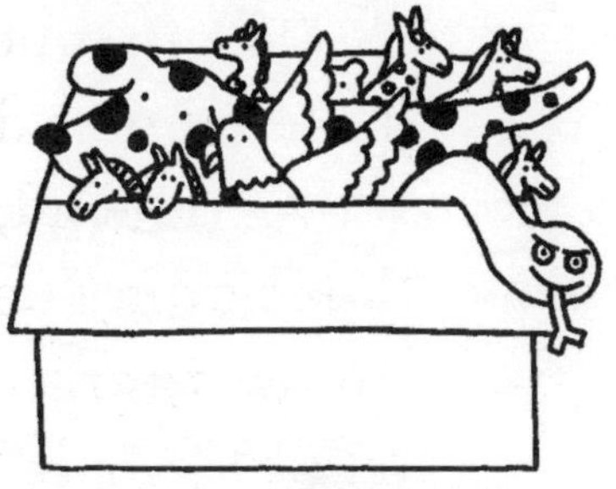

'Look, guys,' I said, squatting down beside the biggest box. 'Want to see my new Mighty Mart comic strip?'

They couldn't see it properly, caged up in the box like that. Wilma Whale couldn't even take a peep because she was rolled up right at the bottom of the box. I heard her calling mournfully to me, making little humpback clicks and bleats.

'It's time you surfaced, Wilma,' I said, though I'd promised to keep all my toys packed up tidily until Dad finished the shelf unit. But he seemed to be taking for ever, and my poor creatures were positively *clamouring* to get out. I tipped up the box quick, and they came stampeding out in a joyous rush.

I let them have a little exercise to ease their crumpled limbs. My horses galloped across the vast pink prairie, Jumper rolled into a dark corner, Wilma leaped right out of the ocean and spouted copiously, Basil slithered across the black jungle, Percy sought out succulent ants under the dressing table, and Polly spread her wings and flew up to the glittering black planet above. She knocked it a little skew-whiff. I very much hoped she hadn't done it any serious damage.

'There now, everyone, freedom at last,' I said. 'OK, I'll show you my latest Mighty Mart adventure. You'll absolutely love it. It's chock-full of animals – amazing fierce polar bears and funny little penguins – and Mighty Mart saves the day, as always.'

I knelt in the middle of the room and read it out to them, showing them each picture, and doing all the different voices, growling and quacking and zapping. I was so absorbed I didn't hear Melissa patter along the landing to the toilet. But *she* heard *me*.

'You sound like a total nutcase!' she said, putting her head round the door. Then she started yelling. 'What are you *doing*? You've got your grotty old animals all over my room!'

'It's *my* room too now. I'm just telling them a story. They got bored being stuffed in that box.'

'You're the weirdest nutter ever! Put them *back*!' said Melissa, gathering them up and tossing them back in the box head first.

'Stop it! You're hurting them!' I said.

'Don't be stupid. How can they get hurt? They're just old rags and plastic. And what on earth's *this*?' Melissa snatched at poor Percy and stared at him. 'I *wondered* where that hairbrush went – I've been looking everywhere for it. *And* the comb. Look what you've done to it – it's totally filthy!'

'He's my porcupine now.'

'No, it's my *hairbrush*.' She started attacking Percy, pulling his soft little body away from his prickles.

'Stop it, you're hurting him terribly!' I said, trying to grab her.

'Don't you dare touch me! We're not allowed to fight, you know that,' said Melissa.

'I know, but I don't care,' I said, and I pushed her.

It was only a little push, but she was bending over and it unbalanced her. She toppled backwards onto her bottom. It made her jerk her head up – and she saw

Polly trying to perch on the lopsided light.

'Oh no! You've broken my chandelier! You hateful *pig*!' Melissa wailed. 'Mum! Mum, look – see what Marty's done now!'

'You mean tell-tale!' I said.

I hoped that Mum might be too busy sewing to come and investigate. I hoped in vain.

'What are you two girls up to now?' she called crossly, and came into our bedroom. 'Are you fighting *again*?' she said. 'What on earth are you playing at, Martina? I told you to keep all your old toys in those boxes until Dad's finished the shelf unit.'

'Can't I even *play* now?'

'Of course you can – but play with your animals one at a time.'

'*Look*, Mum!' said Melissa, pointing upwards dramatically.

Mum looked. 'Oh, Martina, you're the giddy limit!' she said.

'She's broken it!' Melissa wailed. 'She did it deliberately.'

'No I didn't! Polly just wanted somewhere to perch,' I said.

'Stop shouting, both of you,' said Mum. 'Wait here while I go and get the kitchen steps.'

'You've ruined my room already,' Melissa hissed.

'You've ruined my entire life,' I retorted.

'You just spoilt everything,' said Melissa, *kicking* poor Basil off the furry black rug.

'Stop attacking him! You're hurting him!'

'It's not a "him", it's a manky bundle of old tights and it looks horrible.'

'He thinks *you* look horrible – and he despises you for telling tales. Mind he doesn't creep out in the middle of the night and wind himself round your neck and choke you to death!' I threatened.

'Yeah, and *he'd* better watch out I don't take my extra-sharp scissors and cut off his silly head,' said Melissa.

Mum came sighing up the stairs with the kitchen steps. She climbed up them, unhooked Polly, and gave the chandelier a little tug and a twist.

'There!' she said. 'It's all right, Melissa. It isn't broken. It just needed straightening.'

'See!' I said.

'But you must never put your parrot up on any light fitting ever again, Martina,' said Mum, climbing down the ladder.

'I didn't put her anywhere, she flew there,' I said, reaching for Polly.

Mum held her out of my grasp. 'Stop that pretending now. You're too old for all these silly games. And listen, it's *dangerous* putting any toy near a light bulb. They get very hot. Your wretched parrot could get singed. It might even catch fire,' she said.

'Oh no! I won't let her go near one ever again,' I said, snatching her back and cradling her in my arms.

'Just put all those animals back in the box and come and help Melissa and me sew your cushions,' said Mum.

I didn't want to sew silly old cushions, but Mum insisted. I was given a great big piece of black velvet and shown how to sew up the side.

'Very neatly now,' said Mum. 'See how carefully Melissa's doing hers.'

I poked my tongue out at Melissa when Mum bent over the poppy costume. Then

I sewed. And sewed and sewed and sewed. It was incredibly boring – until the black velvet started moving and I realized it was turning into a huge great blobby black bear. I couldn't give him proper arms or

legs or a head, but I took some red cotton and sewed him very small eyes and a nose and a mouth in one corner, so at least he had a face.

I kept the top bunk, of course. I shared with Wilma Whale and Basil and half of Percy. I wanted to share with everyone, but Jumper took up too much room and the horses were too hard and Polly kept on pecking me.

Melissa had the bottom bunk with Baba. She made out she was so grown up and sophisticated, and sneered at all my animals, but she took a baby rag doll to bed with her each night. The doll really *was*

in rags now and her pink towelling face had gone yellowy with age. Melissa kept Baba hidden under her pillow all day and only took her out at bedtime because she needed her to get to sleep. Melissa wasn't very keen on sleepovers with her friends because she couldn't take Baba with her in case they laughed.

Mum tried to get her to throw Baba out. Melissa decided to do it once, and actually put Baba in the dustbin – but in the middle of the night she started crying, and Dad had to go outside in his dressing gown and slippers and rescue Baba before the rubbish lorry came.

Mum and Dad came into our room to kiss us goodnight. Dad kissed Wilma and Basil and half of Percy too. He would have kissed Baba, but Melissa kept her lurking beneath her covers. No one knew she was there. Except me.

'Night-night, girls. Sleep well,' said Mum.

'Night-night, sleep tight. Don't let the bugs bite,' said Dad. We haven't *got* bugs. He always says that, just to be silly.

They switched off the light and crept out, as if we were babies about to fall asleep. But Melissa and I were both wide awake.

'I *hate* this bunk bed! There's nowhere near enough room,' said Melissa, wriggling around.

'There's *heaps* of room,' I said. I paused. 'So long as you're a thin person.'

'Are you suggesting I'm *fat*?' said Melissa, sounding horrified.

I grinned in the dark. Melissa isn't the slightest bit fat, but she worries she might be. She often peers at herself anxiously in the mirror, sucking in her tummy and pulling silly faces to make her cheeks look hollow.

'I'm not a bit fat. You're not allowed to call me that, Mum said. You'll give me that

eating disease. I'll tell on you if you don't watch out,' said Melissa.

'Do you know the one type of person I hate and despise more than anything – a tell-tale,' I said. 'Tell-tale tit, your tongue shall be split, and all the little doggies will have a little bit.'

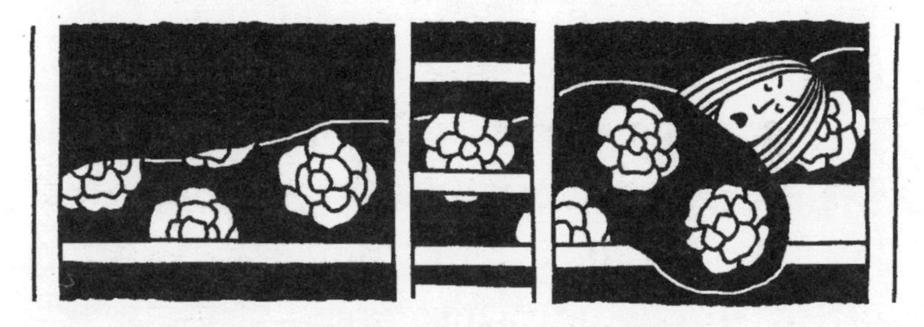

'That's a pathetically stupid rhyme. You're such a baby,' said Melissa.

'*I'm* not the one all tucked up with my baby doll,' I said.

'I'm *not* tucked up. I can't get my duvet to go right in this stupid bunk bed,' said Melissa, heaving herself around.

'Keep *still*, you're rocking me about. You'll tip the bunk beds over if you're not careful,' I said.

Melissa moved more cautiously. 'They wouldn't *really* tip, would they?' she said.

'They might. They very nearly tipped right over once, when I tried jumping up and down on the top bunk.'

'Yes, well, surprise surprise – of course they'd tip then. No wonder they're so rickety, with you leaping about like a monkey.'

'I wish I had a monkey. Hey, Mighty Mart could turn into Mighty Monkey in the jungle and grow a beautiful long tail and swing from branch to branch.'

'Yes, and you could grow one of those rude red monkey bottoms too,' said Melissa, sniggering.

'You shut up. Yes, Mighty Mart is deep in the jungle and she's thrusting her way through the undergrowth. It's boiling hot and the mosquitoes are nipping her, but she doesn't flinch. She strides onwards in her Converse boots, but then she hears something!'

'What?'

'Ssh, she's listening! She hears this *rustle-rustle-rustle*. Something's gliding towards her, nearer and nearer. The jungle birds stop their squawking, the animals all hide, because *something* is coming!'

'*What?*'

'It's a massive boa constrictor – an evil creature that can kill you with one clasp. Even Mighty Mart is powerless if he chooses to strike.'

As I spoke, I uncoiled Basil and very slowly hung him down from my top bunk.

'Yes, the boa constrictor strikes terror in everyone's hearts. Watch out – he's coming, he's coming!'

I leaned right over and shook Basil so that he brushed Melissa's face. She screamed and shot out of bed, shaking her arms and legs, fighting thin air.

'Watch out, he's going to get little Baba now,' I said, choking with laughter.

'No he's *not*!' said Melissa, clutching her shabby old doll.

'Melissa!' Mum came rushing into our bedroom. 'What's happened? What's the matter? Why are you out of bed?'

'She's fine, Mum. We were just playing,' I said, pulling Basil back into my bunk.

'Well, *don't* play! It's time to go to sleep. And don't either of you scream like that. You sounded really frightened,' said Mum.

'Melissa *was* really frightened,' I said triumphantly as Mum went back to her sewing.

'No I wasn't,' said Melissa sullenly, getting back into bed with Baba.

'Yes you were! Scared stiff of Basil, even though you say he's just a manky bundle of old tights. Oh, you nearly got her, didn't you, Basil my boy. Watch out, Melissa. He'll wait until you're fast asleep – and then he'll come slithering down again.'

'And I'll rip him to shreds – I'm warning you,' said Melissa. 'Now shut up, Marty. Go to sleep.'

'I'm not the slightest bit sleepy. It feels so weird being in this room. It *smells*.'

'It does not!'

'Yes, it does – it smells of your horrible hand cream.'

'That's a *lovely* smell.'

'It truly pongs. It's making me cough – listen!' I coughed loudly. I made Wilma and Basil and Jumper and Polly and Half-Percy and all six horses cough too.

'This is a madhouse,' said Melissa, burrowing right under her duvet.

'No, it's a jungle, and all the animals are sick and coughing with deadly rose pollutant. They're all keeling over and dying – *listen*.' I made every single creature flop onto their back, gasping.

'I'm not listening,' Melissa said, from deep under her duvet.

I made up a glorious adventure about Mighty Mart striding into the jungle with a big mask over her face. She sprayed all the rose pollutant until it evaporated into pink clouds that floated away. Melissa clearly *wasn't* listening, because she started snoring.

I giggled at first, hearing my prim, fussy sister making such silly snorty-pig sounds, but after a while it started to get annoying. *I* wanted to get to sleep, but how could I when there was this piglet in the bunk below?

'Melissa!' I leaned right down from my top bunk and gave her a prod. 'Melissa, wake up!'

'What?' Melissa mumbled.

'You're snoring!'

'No I'm not!'

'Well you're not right this *second* because I've just woken you up.'

'So shut up. I *don't* snore anyway,' said Melissa.

She burrowed down in her bunk bed. In less than a minute she was snoring again, even louder this time.

I pulled my own duvet right over my head, and curled up with my animals and whispered Mighty Mart stories to them. I didn't get to sleep for *ages* – but it helped me come up with a cunning plan to get my own back on Katie and Ingrid.

I got up very early the next morning, as soon as I heard Mum go into the bathroom. I whizzed downstairs into the kitchen. I opened up the fridge and peered inside.

I was momentarily distracted by the leftover trifle on the bottom shelf. My finger reached out all by itself and started scraping up the cream, and a cherry or two, *and* it scooped a peach slice out of the sponge – but then I managed to get it under control again. I left the trifle alone and reached for an egg box. I shook it gently to make sure it was full, and then sneaked it back upstairs, carrying it under my pyjama top just in case I bumped into Mum or Dad.

Melissa was still sound asleep on the bottom bunk, so I wrapped the egg box carefully in two old T-shirts for protection and put it in my school bag. There! Mission accomplished!

I was a little unnerved at breakfast when Mum was unusually nice.

'How did you get on sharing, girls?' she asked, giving us both a hug. 'Did you go to sleep quickly after all that squeaking and squealing?'

'One of us did,' I said, spooning cornflakes into my mouth. 'The one of us who snores like a pig.'

'I *don't*!' said Melissa indignantly.

'Of course you don't,' said Dad. 'No one in this family snores. We just breathe deeply, don't we?'

That made me giggle and choke on my cornflakes, because Dad snores *terribly*. He doesn't sound like a piglet, he sounds more like a great snorty *warthog*.

'Careful with those cornflakes, Martina,' said Mum. She spread her hands, waggling her fingers about. 'I sewed the last cushion last night, *and* finished the poppy costume. And one of the Year Five mums emailed. Her oldest daughter's getting married and she wants me to tackle her wedding dress and three bridesmaid's dresses too.'

'But you're already doing another lot of bridesmaid's dresses, aren't you? You can't take on *too* much, love. Your hands are playing up as it is,' said Dad.

'No, I'm fine. They don't need these dresses for months yet. And guess what! One of the dancing-school mums wants a blue dress just like Martina's for her daughter.' She patted my curls. 'You were a brilliant little model for me, sweetheart.'

'A rhapsody in blue,' said Dad.

'Bluebottle, more like,' said Melissa.

I felt myself flushing. Were all the Year Sixes calling me Bluebottle too? They didn't even know me.

'How did you know?' I hissed.

'I heard that Katie and Ingrid calling after you,' Melissa whispered. She paused. 'Do you want me and my friends to sort them out for you?'

'No thanks. *I'll* sort them out, don't worry,' I said.

'What are you two whispering about?' said Mum.

'Just . . . secrets,' I said.

'There! I *knew* sharing a room would bring you closer together,' Mum said happily. She looked at her watch. 'We're quite early for once. You were very good to get up without being called, Martina. There's just about time for me to cook you a proper breakfast if you'd like. What about bacon and eggs?'

Eggs!

'No thanks,' I said quickly. 'I'm full of cornflakes.'

'No thanks, Mum,' said Melissa, luckily. 'Fried breakfasts are sooo fattening.'

'No thanks, Jan. I'm going out for an hour or two, leafleting the neighbourhood,' said Dad.

He'd designed a little advert for his travel services on the computer and was eager to spread the word about. And *I* was eager to spread my eggs about. I sat all through morning lessons fingering the box in my school bag. I waited for lunch time, when they'd have maximum impact. Then I went strolling out into the playground, where all the girls were starting up a new rounders game. Katie had made herself captain. Ingrid and Alisha and everyone else wanted to be on *her* team.

'I'll be captain of the *other* team,' I said.

'No you won't. You're not even playing,' said Katie. 'No one wants to play with you, Bluebottle.'

'Yeah, push off, Bluebottle,' said Ingrid.

'You're rubbish, Bluebottle,' said Alisha.

Several other girls started up a Bluebottle chant. Some of the boys started peering in our direction, distracted from their own game. I didn't care if the whole playground was watching. I smiled and swung my school bag purposefully.

'What are you grinning at, Bluebottle?' asked Katie.

'Do you know what bluebottles *are*?' I said.

'Of course I do,' said Katie. 'They're *you*!'

'You haven't a clue what a *real* bluebottle is, have you?'

'It's an insect,' said Ingrid. 'A horrible creepy-crawly insect.'

'Yeah, like *you*,' said Alisha.

'*I'm* not the creepy-crawly one, grubbing and grovelling to Katie. That's you two. If I'm a bluebottle, that means I'm a blowfly.'

'So? Blowflies are horrible,' said Ingrid.

'*They're* not horrible, they're just little insects, but the stuff they lay their eggs in is *ever* so horrible – rotting meat, dung and dead things and wounds. That's what you lot are – rotting and smelly and dead and all-over pus. So I'm going to lay my eggs in you.' I reached into my school bag, got out the egg box, opening it up in a trice, and started throwing them.

I have a terrific aim. I got Katie right on the head, so the egg went all over her long hair. I got Ingrid on the nose, splat all down her face. And I got Alisha right in the middle of her big fat tummy, so the egg slid off her skirt and dripped all the way down her legs. I still had three more eggs, but Katie started *running* towards the girls' toilets, blubbing like a baby. Ingrid ran after her, jabbering, 'We're telling! We're telling!' And Alisha ran too, having to hop and skip because her skirt was so soggy.

Everyone else stood stock-still, staring at me, mouths open.

'Anyone else want to call me Bluebottle?' I said.

There were no takers at all. They just gazed at me in awe, as if I had turned into Mighty Mart.

'Wow!' said Micky West, walking over with all his boy gang around him. 'That showed them!'

'You can't half throw good, Marty!' said Simon Mason.

'Their faces!' said Jeremy Wymark.

They started laughing, and most of the other boys joined in. The girls still looked a bit stunned.

'You'll be for it now, Marty,' Mandy Heart said anxiously.

'Look – they've told *Mr Hubbard*!' said Julie Brown.

I looked where she was pointing. Yes,

there was Mr Hubbard himself, our headteacher, red in the face, marching purposefully towards me. And he wasn't alone. He had our school secretary with him. Mrs Michaels. My mum.

If I really was Mighty Mart I'd give a cheery wave to everyone and leap into the air, flying up into the sky now that I'd sorted out the bullies. But I wasn't Mighty Mart. I was me – and I stayed rooted to the spot.

I was in trouble. Big-time. I was frog-marched into school and given a severe lecture in Mr Hubbard's room while Mum cleaned up Katie and Ingrid and Alisha, who were all in tears.

'I can't believe you could behave so badly, Martina,' said Mr Hubbard. 'Throwing eggs is not only an unpleasant, hostile, stupid thing to do, it's also dangerous. You could have really hurt Katie or Ingrid or Alisha.'

I'd *wanted* to hurt them, but I had enough sense not to say that out loud.

'It was an entirely unprovoked attack by all accounts,' said Mr Hubbard. 'What possessed you to do such a thing? And *why* were you carrying six raw eggs around in your school bag?'

I wondered about telling him the Bluebottle tale, but knew he wouldn't understand. So I just stood there, staring at his desk, shifting my weight from one foot to the other, while he droned on and on. It wasn't really dreadful at all, just boring. But I knew this was simply the lull before the storm. The storm was Mum.

When the bell rang for afternoon school, Mr Hubbard waved me away. I galloped smartly down the corridor, but Mum shot out of her office, charged after me, and had her hands clamped on my shoulders before I could escape.

She gave me a little shake. 'Just wait till I get you home!' she hissed.

It was very strange doing lessons that afternoon. I had very hard sums and then a spelling test, usually my two worst things, but I wanted each lesson to go on for ever. Our teacher, Mrs Madley, had been told all about the Egg Incident and felt it necessary to give me another little lecture in front of the whole class – though her lips kept quivering, almost as if she were about to burst out laughing. Perhaps it was the sight of Katie and Ingrid and Alisha. Mum had done her best, but they still looked very eggy, especially Katie. It looked as if she hadn't washed her hair for weeks. They all glared at me, naturally, but they didn't try to poke me in the back, and though they whispered to each other, they didn't say the dreaded word Bluebottle, not once.

The other kids were still staring at me warily, clearly wondering what I was going to do next. Micky West sent me a note!

Dear Marty

You are ace at throwing eggs!!! You're good at rounders too. You can be on my team tomorrow if you want.

Micky

My heart soared. The boys never ever let girls play on their teams. But here was Micky *inviting* me to play with them!

I wrote back:

Dear Micky

That would be cool.

Marty

and added a smiley face.

I wasn't sure I'd be in a fit state to play rounders tomorrow though. I was sure Mum was going to beat me up.

It was actually *worse*. She kept ominously quiet all the way home, and only got started when we were inside our front door.

'I have never been so ashamed in all my life,' she said. 'Go up to your bedroom this instant, Martina. I can't bear to look at you.'

I didn't have my own bedroom any more. I had to languish in the pink room, marooned on my top bunk. I wrapped Wilma Whale around me and sucked my thumb. I was starving hungry. We always had fruit smoothies and biscuits when we got home from school. It was clear that I was going to have to go without. I searched my school bag for forgotten biscuits or toffees, but couldn't find so much as a crumb or an empty wrapper.

'I don't care,' I declared defiantly. 'Mighty Mart sometimes doesn't eat for days and days. In fact, when she's on a particular mission to save this planet, she's so busy she doesn't have time to eat at all. She just gets thinner and thinner and thinner until she's as thin as an arrow, but that's all to the good because she shoots herself way up into the stratosphere. If any of her arch enemies get near her and fire their deadly weapons, she's so narrow they can't spot her in their targets and miss her completely.'

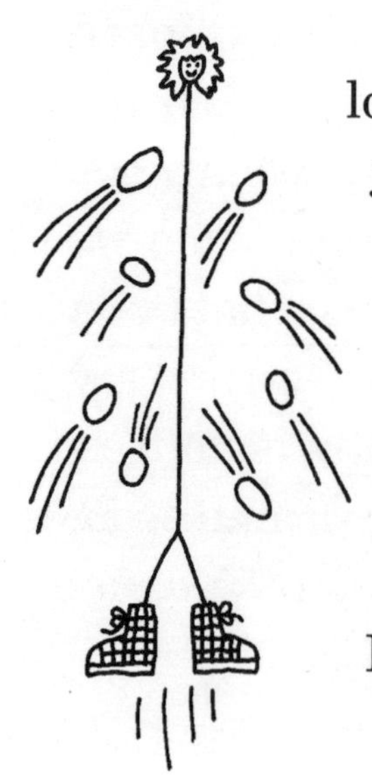

I drew Mighty Mart as one long line down my page, with just a tiny pinhead on top and two Converse boots at the bottom. I added a lot of bullets and bombs flying all around her – but they started to look like eggs. I added little stick-people Katie and Ingrid and Alisha, and pelted them all over again. I got my yellow felt pen and made them positively *drip* with egg. I laughed and laughed – but it was a hyena laugh, and it didn't sound right.

'What are you laughing at?' said Dad, coming into the room.

'Oh, Dad!' I said, and I jumped down from my bunk bed and ran into his arms.

But something was wrong. He didn't hug me back or swing me round and round. He just *stood* there. I peered up at him.

'Dad?'

I dug at his tummy with my chin. He didn't respond.

'Curlynob?' I said, reaching for his hand to pat my curls.

But Dad pushed me away, gently but firmly. 'Come on now, Martina.'

'Marty!'

'This isn't just one of your usual silly pranks. You're in very serious trouble. And it's no laughing matter,' said Dad.

'I wasn't laughing. Not really,' I said.

'I just *heard* you. And what's this?' He seized my sketchbook and saw the bright yellow splats and scribbles all over the page. 'For pity's sake, you're revelling in this! What on earth's got into you? Mum's in tears downstairs, she's so upset. How could you ever do such a thing to those poor girls?'

'They're not poor girls, Dad. They've been really mean to Marty, calling her this daft name,' said Melissa, peeping round the door.

I stared at my sister in astonishment.

'That's enough, Melissa. Go back downstairs,' said Dad.

'But it's *true*, Dad. It isn't Marty's fault. They were all turning against her. I should have helped her, but she said she didn't want me to,' said Melissa. She looked really upset, as if she might start crying. Like me.

'Melissa. Please. Go downstairs,' said Dad.

She did as she was told.

'Are you really, really cross with me, Dad?' I whispered.

'Yes I am,' said Dad.

I tried to pull Wilma over my head, but he pulled her off me.

'Now then, stop your cute baby tricks – I know you're just trying to get round me,' he said. 'It's time you grew up a bit. All right, I dare say you felt you had to stand up to these girls. Was it the ones you go on about – Katie and Ingrid?'

'Yes. And Alisha.'

'Is she the plump girl who had one of Mum's dresses? Honestly, that poor little soul didn't look as if she could say boo to a goose. Now, Melissa says these girls were teasing you . . . What names were they calling you?'

I shook my head.

'Come on. Tell me. I need to know.' Dad paused. 'Was it a rude name? Look, *spell* it out.'

'B-L-U-E-B-O-T-T-L-E,' I mumbled.

Dad screwed up his face. 'Bluebottle?' he repeated incredulously. 'Oh, good Lord! I can't believe this. That's not *rude*!'

'They're ever so rude to me,' I said. 'Well, they *were*. But they won't be any more.'

'I don't care *what* they call you – bluebottle, wasp, bumblebee–' Dad snorted, almost as if he might turn back into *my* dad and start laughing.

I smiled at him hopefully but he frowned back at me.

'I told you, it isn't the slightest bit funny. You could have seriously hurt those girls.'

'It was only eggs, Dad.'

'They could have gone in their eyes, or a piece of shell could have cut them. You've no idea what damage you could have done. It's a horrible, disgusting thing to do. Mum said those poor girls were terribly upset. Goodness knows what their mothers will say. And can't you see how embarrassing this is for Mum, when she's the school secretary? And Alisha's mother had just ordered a brand-new dress.' Dad paused. 'Aren't you even going to say sorry?'

'I'm sorry,' I mumbled, because I was very, very, very sorry Dad was so mad at me.

'That's better,' he said.

'Can I come downstairs now?'

'No, not yet. You need to think things over quietly, and make up your mind that you'll never ever do anything so silly again.'

So I thought things over for a very long time, while my tummy rumbled miserably. Then I started to sniff wonderful *supper* smells. I was almost sure it was macaroni cheese,

one of my special favourites. Mum and Dad would have to call me down when they dished up. I heard Mum in the kitchen. I listened to the thump of the oven door, the clatter of crockery, the hiss of the tap as she filled up the water glasses.

'Oh yes!' I murmured, rubbing my tummy.

And 'Oh no!' I wailed when I heard the three of them chomping away downstairs, eating their macaroni cheese *without me*.

Mum and Dad were leaving me stuck upstairs to *starve*. I flung myself on my face on my top bunk and started sobbing bitterly, so much that I didn't even hear Mum come in . . . with a tray of supper for me!

'At least you're starting to understand just how naughty you've been,' said Mum. 'Sit up now, Martina. Oh dear, have you got a tissue? Let's blow that nose. Now, calm down and have some supper.'

At least I was getting *my* plate of macaroni cheese. Unfortunately Mum stayed while I ate it, and she lectured me as I chewed every golden mouthful.

'When you've finished, you're going to write three letters, young lady. One to Katie, one to Ingrid, and one to Alisha. You're going to apologize profusely to each girl.'

'Oh, *Mum*! I bet *they* won't apologize for being mean to me.'

'That's beside the point,' said Mum. 'And it doesn't sound as if they were *very* mean, anyway. They called you Bluebottle, is that right? Well it's a rather silly name, but it's not really nasty, now is it? Why Bluebottle anyway? Is it because you buzz about?'

'No! It's because I had to wear that blue dress to Alisha's party,' I said piteously.

'Oh! Well, that's silly, because you looked lovely in the blue dress – everyone said so.

Did they call Alisha names because of *her* dress?'

'No, because she sucks up to them. They don't like me. They say I'm weird,' I said.

I'd cheered up quite considerably because the macaroni cheese was extra good, with lovely crispy cheesy bits – but Mum suddenly looked as if she was going to burst out crying again.

'Do they really say you're weird?' she said.

'Well, yes. But I don't mind,' I said.

'*I* mind,' said Mum. 'Oh, Martina, *why* won't you try and fit in more? You're an intelligent little girl. If you'd only play nicely with the others and stop all your silly pretend games, you'd fit in easily enough and make friends.'

'I've *got* friends,' I said. 'Jaydene's my *best* friend.'

'Yes, and she seems a very sweet girl,

but you haven't got any other friends, have you?'

'Yes I have. I made a brand-new friend today who wants to play with me tomorrow at lunch time.'

'Really?' said Mum. 'Who?'

'Micky West.'

'But he's a boy,' said Mum, as if he didn't count.

'Lots of the boys like me,' I said.

'Yes, well, that's good – but you're a *girl*, Martina. I wish you weren't such a terrible tomboy. Listen, would you really like to go to Miss Suzanne's dancing class? Maybe you could make some new friends there.'

'I think I've gone off that idea now, Mum. I'm *fine*. I don't *want* to be friends with girls like Katie and Ingrid and Alisha. I *like* being weird.'

'Oh, Martina.' Mum sighed deeply. 'I wish you weren't so stubborn.'

'You wish I was more like Melissa, don't you?' I said.

‘Nooo, not exactly,’ said Mum, struggling. ‘I mean, you’re *you* – you’re a lovely girl in many ways. I think it’s wonderful that you have such a good imagination and that you’re so artistic, but I wish you’d use your gifts more . . . productively. You could do some really lovely drawings and paintings if you tried, but you waste your time with those silly comic pictures.’

‘Mighty Mart isn’t silly!’

Mum picked up my sketchbook and frowned at thin-as-a-pin Mighty Mart throwing her eggs. ‘This scribble is just a waste of crayons and paper,’ she said. ‘You haven’t even drawn her properly. And what is she supposed to be doing?’

I kept a cautious silence.

‘She’s not . . . throwing eggs, is she?’ said Mum. She went pink in the face again.

‘No, no, she’s . . . she’s in Sunshine Land, and those are all the little sunbeams,’ I said.

Mum rolled her eyes – and I can't say I blamed her.

She went to get her own notepaper and envelopes, and then stood over me while I wrote letters of apology.

'Can't I at least use the computer and print it out three times?' I said.

'No, you're going to do this the polite, old-fashioned way. I want the other mothers to see you've been brought up properly, even though you've done such a dreadful thing,' said Mum.

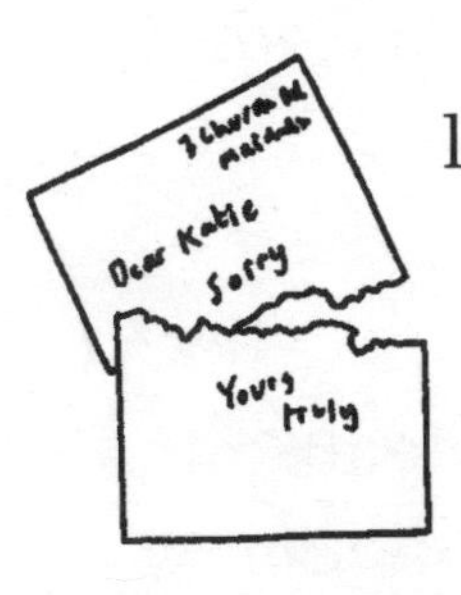

So I had to write three terrible letters, resting on my supper tray. *Four*, because Mum rejected my first letter out of hand. '*Dear Katie, sorry. Yours truly*,' she read out in disgust, and then ripped it in two. 'Do it properly this time!'

'But I said sorry!'

'You certainly don't *sound* sorry. I'll dictate the letter. Come on, start again, with your address in the top right-hand corner.'

'This is so *boring*,' I moaned.

Dear Katie

I am very sorry I threw an egg at you in the playground. It was a very silly thing to do. My parents are very cross with me. I do hope it didn't hurt you too much or spoil your clothes. I promise I will never do such a silly thing again.

Yours sincerely
Martina Michaels

Then I had to do the same again for Ingrid, and yet another for Alisha. Sorry, sorry, grovel grovel. For the first time ever I didn't mind signing myself Martina.

It was too shaming a letter for Marty to sign.

When Mum had gone at last, I picked up an *invisible* pen and wrote all over each letter: *No, I'm not the slightest bit sorry, you mean, hateful pig*. You couldn't *see* the writing, of course, but it made me feel much better to know it was there.

I wasn't allowed to come downstairs at all, right up until bedtime. It was probably the longest evening of my life. I drew Mighty Mart and played with my animals, but it seemed very strange being stuck upstairs in isolation when I could hear the television and all the family noises downstairs.

Mum and Dad eventually came upstairs when it was Melissa's bedtime. I pretended to be asleep. I huddled down with Wilma wrapped around my head and breathed heavily in and out. Mum and Dad talked to me, but I made out I couldn't hear them. They kissed me goodnight, though it was just *one* kiss, and Dad didn't say, 'Night-night, sleep tight, don't let the bugs bite.'

I snuffled into Wilma.

'You're not really asleep, are you, Marty?' Melissa whispered.

The bunk beds creaked and she climbed the ladder up to my top bunk.

'Hey! I think they were mean to you. Did you really have to write letters of apology?' she asked.

'Yes! And Mum's going to come with me tomorrow to make sure I hand them out and it's going to be mega-humiliating,' I said mournfully.

'Oh, you poor thing,' said Melissa.

She climbed right up onto my top bunk. I normally wouldn't allow this. The top bunk is *my* territory. But tonight it was very comforting indeed to be cuddled up with Melissa, who seemed to be the only member of my family who still loved me.

When we woke up we were still cuddled up together, which felt very weird indeed. Then Melissa threw Wilma the Whale out of bed because she said she was smothering her, and I dug her in the ribs accidentally-on-purpose, and we were soon back to normal, having a row.

It was a terrible morning because I had to give Katie and Ingrid and Alisha their letters of apology. I actually had to *say* sorry too, with Mum prompting me fiercely. Then Jaydene saw me handing out the letters

and got entirely the wrong end of the stick. She thought they were party invitations and was terribly upset, thinking I was inviting all my worst enemies but totally ignoring my best friend forever.

'Don't be crazy, Jaydene. As if! I'd never invite Katie or Ingrid or Alisha to a party in a million years. Not unless it was a torture party, and we played real Murder in the Dark.'

'So can I really come to your party, Marty?' said Jaydene, her big brown eyes shining.

'But I'm not *having* a party. It's not my birthday for ages yet,' I said. 'And Mum says our house is too small for proper parties anyway. We're just allowed to have a few friends, that's all.'

'So I can come, then, as I'm your BFF?' said Jaydene.

'But I'm not . . .' I gave up. 'OK, I'll ask Mum,' I said, though I didn't hold out much hope of her letting me, seeing as she thought I was the worst daughter ever.

Jaydene gave me a great bit grateful hug, which felt good. The day started picking up a bit after that – and lunch time was magic. I went and played rounders with the boys! We didn't even call it rounders – it was American baseball, which sounded much cooler. We all had to give each other mad names, like real American baseball players.

'I'm Tricky Micky,' said Micky West.

'I'm Simon Pieman,' said Simon Mason.

'I'm Jeremy Brown the Clown,' said Jeremy Brown.

'OK, I'm Farty Marty,' I said, which made them all crack up laughing.

We played this really ace game, and they all cheered when I got my first home run. Mum kept coming out into the playground and peering anxiously at me. She looked horrified when she heard Micky and his gang calling me by my brilliant new nickname. She caught hold of me when the bell went for afternoon school.

'*What* were they calling you, Martina?' she asked.

'Farty Marty,' I said proudly.

Mum gasped. 'But that's *much* worse than Bluebottle!'

'No it's not. And *I'm* calling me that, so it's absolutely cool. The boys all like me, Mum,' I said, trying to reassure her.

'But what about the girls?' said Mum.

'Well . . . Jaydene likes me,' I said. 'Mum, can Jaydene come to tea? A fancy tea, like a little party?'

'Oh, Martina, I'm so busy just now. I haven't got time to do anything fancy.'

'*I'll* do it.'

'As if I'd let you loose in my kitchen!'

'*Please* let me have Jaydene round, Mum.' I had a sudden inspiration. 'I want to show her our lovely new bedroom.'

That did the trick. I was allowed to invite Jaydene to tea on Friday – to admire my new bedroom.

'But I thought you said you hated it, Marty,' said Jaydene.

'Yes, I do. I'm just using it as a *ploy*,' I said.

Jaydene didn't look as if she understood. 'So is your bedroom horrible or lovely?' she said.

'Horrible. Hideous. Horrendous,' I said.

I especially didn't like it now that Dad had finished the new shelf units. They fitted well and Dad had made them look good, painting each shelf and cupboard glossy white – but they came with appalling new *rules*. I had to keep all my stuff neat and folded and in the right little section. If I shuffled through everything, frantically looking for something vitally important, I had to put everything back in its right place – or else Melissa would tell on me to Mum.

The shelves were a terrible curse too. We were supposed to use them to display our favourite things. Melissa spent an entire evening arranging hers – sorting her books into *alphabetical order*, and lining up her jewellery box, her little flock of angel figurines, her scented candles in little glass jars, and a framed photo of Justin Bieber with *To Melissa, with all my love, Justin* written on it. *He* didn't write it, Melissa did.

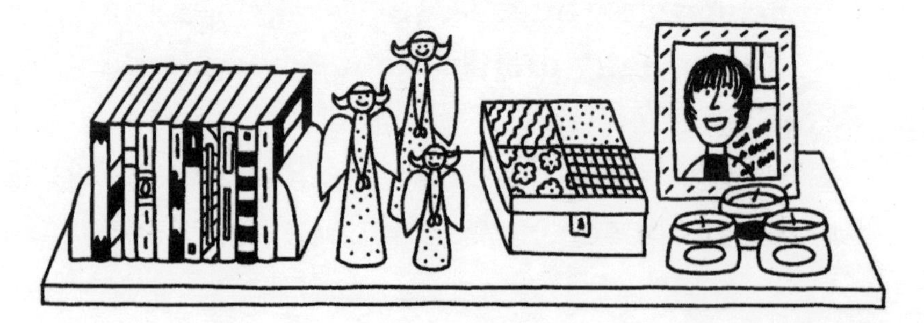

I put my own favourite things on *my* shelf: my sketchbooks, my crayons and felt tips, and my animals – Wilma (carefully folded), Jumper the dog, Basil, Polly Parrot, Half-Percy, and all my horses and their shoe box stable. They splashed and jumped and slithered and flapped and rootled and cantered very happily in their new home, and I was pleased – but Melissa started shrieking.

'Mum! Mum, Marty's spread all her tatty old animals all over her shelf and they look *dreadful*! They're spoiling the whole effect. She's ruining *everything*.'

Mum took Melissa's side, surprise surprise.

'Really, Martina! Dad's gone to all this trouble to make a lovely shelf unit and you're spoiling it already. The shelf is for your *special* things.'

'My animals *are* special!'

'Rubbish! And that's exactly what they *are* – rubbish. I'm not letting you have that lot on show. People will think we've never given you any proper teddies,' said Mum. 'If you *must* hang onto this motley crew, then they have to be kept hidden away in your cupboard space.' She swept them off the shelf with one dramatic gesture.

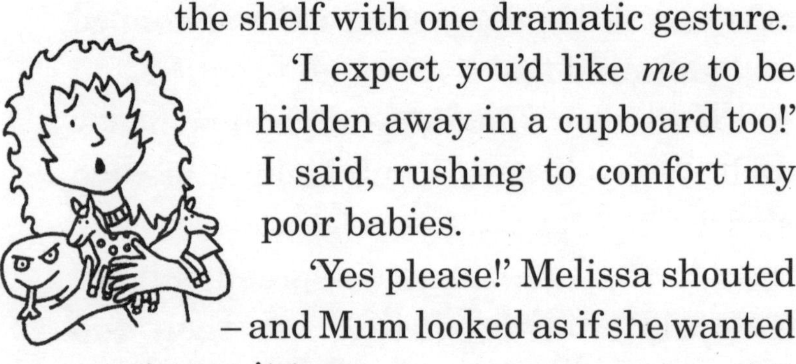

'I expect you'd like *me* to be hidden away in a cupboard too!' I said, rushing to comfort my poor babies.

'Yes please!' Melissa shouted – and Mum looked as if she wanted to say it too.

'Now, now, don't all gang up on little Mart,' said Dad. He was back to being my lovely, funny, *kind* dad now, thank goodness. 'I can't see why she can't have her animals on the shelf if that's what she wants.'

'Yay!' I yelled triumphantly, gathering up my animals. 'Dad made the shelves, so he gets to say what we put on them, *see*!'

'But then we *all* have to see them and they look ridiculous,' said Melissa, practically crying.

That's the worst thing about my sister. She's two and a half years older than me, but whenever she can't get her own way she starts boo-hooing like a baby, and Mum and Dad give in to her.

'How about a compromise, Marty?' said Dad. 'Wilma likes to sleep in your bunk bed, so let's tuck her up there. Surely Jumper would love a new kennel . . . Look, he's jumping into the cupboard all by himself. Basil would like to lie right underneath the bunk beds in the dark and *lurk*. Polly and this poor little Percy chap look as if they could do with a little lie-down too. There! Now you can spread all your horses out properly on your shelf. Don't they look good?'

I knew perfectly well that I was being conned. I still wanted *all* my animals out on my shelf, but I let Dad sweet-talk me into his compromise. You'd have thought Melissa would have been grateful, but she still moaned. When I decided to give Patches, Gee-Up, Sugarlump, Merrylegs, Dandelion and Starlight some exercise, and set up little fences with my books and crayons, she said I was making my shelf untidy on purpose.

I was *amazed* at Jaydene's reaction to our bedroom when she came after school on Friday. She stood in the doorway and *clapped her hands*!

'It's beautiful!' she said. 'Oh, Marty, you're so *lucky*!'

She tiptoed around the room, gazing at the shelf unit, the duvet covers, the cushions. She gave a little scream of delight when she looked up and saw the

black chandelier. 'It's just wonderful!' she said. 'Oh, I'd give anything in the whole world to have a bedroom like this. It's so pretty, and yet it's not a bit babyish. It's like a bedroom for a grown-up lady.'

'Well, maybe, but I've got hardly any of my stuff out here. It was all so different in my Marty Den. I had this wonderful big old chair and you could play Jumping. It was such *fun*,' I said.

'Didn't you worry you'd get told off? My mum goes nuts if I jump on the furniture,' said Jaydene.

'Yeah, well, it was all broken up so it didn't really matter too much. And I had this old chest and I used one of the drawers as a sledge.'

Jaydene wrinkled up her nose. 'Why would you want to do that, Marty? But this is all *beautiful*. You've got such gorgeous things. I *love* your angels and your candles.'

'They're not mine, they're Melissa's,' I said sullenly.

'Oh, look! She's got a signed photo of Justin Bieber! It says *with all my love*! I can't believe it!'

'She cut it out of a magazine, silly, and wrote on it herself.'

'Well, it's still a lovely photo,' said Jaydene.

She sat down at Melissa's dressing table and touched all her horrible make-up and hand cream with her fingertips. 'Are all these Melissa's too?' she said. 'Is she really allowed to wear make-up? Does she ever let *you* wear any, Marty?'

'Yuck! I don't want to wear make-up! It looks stupid – and it *smells*,' I said.

'It smells lovely in here,' said Jaydene rapturously, breathing in deeply.

'That's Melissa's horrible rose hand cream. Doesn't the smell make your nose go all tickly?'

'No, I think it's beautiful,' said Jaydene.

She fingered the jar delicately. 'Do you think Melissa might let me try just a tiny bit?'

'Yes, go on, help yourself,' I said.

'Oh, I'd better ask her first,' said Jaydene. She went to the sewing room, where Melissa was helping Mum with the costumes. I'd specifically requested that she keep out of our way. But now Jaydene was spoiling everything, because Melissa came back into our room with us and showed Jaydene how to apply her wretched hand cream. Honestly, it's not exactly rocket science: cream, hands, rub!

‘Can I have some too?’ I asked Melissa.

She looked astonished, but said yes.

I took a nice dollop and then started rubbing it on Patches and Gee-Up and Sugarlump and Merrylegs and Dandelion and Starlight to see if it made their coats shine.

‘Marty!’ said Melissa. ‘Don’t waste my hand cream on your stupid horses!’

‘Oh, Marty, you’re so funny!’ Jaydene giggled, rubbing her rose-scented hands together. ‘Mmm, this smells *heavenly*! I feel so grown up.’ She looked at all Melissa’s make-up. ‘Of course, I’d feel even more grown up if I could wear some make-up,’ she said hopefully.

Melissa smiled at her. ‘Would you like me to make you up, Jaydene?’ she asked, in this sweetie-pie, silly-girlie voice, like Glinda the Good Witch in *The Wizard of Oz*.

‘Oh, Melissa, *yes*!’ said Jaydene.

It took *ages*, and Jaydene didn't even want to talk to me while Melissa dabbed all her make-up junk onto her face. Jaydene just listened to Melissa the Beauty Queen. She told her all this utter rubbish about your eye shadow reflecting the colour of your eyes, and kissing a tissue after you've applied your first coat of lipstick. Melissa was making it up as she went along, but Jaydene drank it all in. I couldn't distract her at all. When Mum called out that it was supper time at long, long last, Jaydene started fussing.

'Oh dear, will all my lipstick come off if I eat my supper?' she said.

I started to think she was such an idiot that I didn't really want to be friends with her after all. She wasn't *acting* like my friend, not in the slightest.

It was spaghetti bolognese for supper. I tried to get Jaydene to play my slurp-slurp-slurp game, when you suck each strand up into your mouth without cutting it up. Mum always tells me off when I do this, but I knew she wouldn't moan at Jaydene, as she was our guest. But Jaydene giggled at me fondly and said it looked as if I had lipstick on too – I had orange spaghetti sauce all round my mouth. She tried to copy the way Melissa ate, winding her spaghetti round and round her fork in an affected manner.

Mum and Dad kept chatting to Jaydene while I fidgeted and sucked and slurped. I wanted them to like her, but it was irritating the way they kept nodding triumphantly at me when Jaydene said I was so lucky to have such a lovely bedroom, and even luckier to have a big sister like Melissa.

We still had about an hour left to play after supper. I was planning to show Jaydene all my Mighty Mart comics and maybe suggest we act one out together. I was even going to invent a brand-new character with superpowers: Giant Jay, who would have her very own adventure.

But Jaydene asked if Melissa would come and play with us too.

'No, we don't want *her*,' I said quickly.

'Yes we do,' said Jaydene.

Melissa didn't *have* to come. But she seemed intent on stealing my best friend away from me. 'Of course I'll come,' she said. 'Let's all go up to my bedroom.'

'It's *my* bedroom too,' I said, but they weren't even listening to me.

They started playing a new, incredibly boring game together – hairdressers!

Melissa twiddled Jaydene's funny little plaits enviously. 'How do you get your hair in those little plaits all over your head, Jaydene? They're so *neat*.'

'My mum does them for me, or sometimes my gran. It takes ages, but I watch telly while they do it. Do you want me to plait *your* hair, Melissa?'

'Oh, yes please!'

I groaned, unable to believe it.

Jaydene looked at me anxiously. 'I'll plait your hair too, Marty,' she said sweetly.

'No thanks. I can't imagine anything more *boring*,' I said rudely. '*Don't* play hairdressers, Jaydene. Play a proper game with me!'

At school I can nearly always make Jaydene do what I want – but here at home it was as if Melissa had cast a spell on her.

'I'll play in a minute, Marty. I'll just show Melissa how to do my kind of plaits. It's only fair, seeing as she did all my make-up,' she said.

A *minute*! Jaydene spent nearly the entire hour combing and plaiting Melissa's horrible hair. While Jaydene parted and gathered and twisted and plaited, she asked Melissa's advice again and again. She wanted to know silly stuff about make-up and clothes and pop stars. I yawned so much I nearly ended up with lockjaw.

But then she got on to school stuff.

'Do you have any really mean girls like Katie and Ingrid in your class, Melissa?' Jaydene asked.

'Yes. I've got Chantelle and Laura. They're *worse*,' said Melissa.

'So how do you manage when they're mean to you?' Jaydene asked anxiously. 'Marty is soooo brave. She just says mean things back, but I can't ever think of stuff to say. Or she fights them, but I'm hopeless at fighting. I just cry if anyone hits me. Or she throws *eggs* – imagine!'

I perked up at this. I remembered that Jaydene was really a very good friend.

'Yeah, well, that's not the most sensible way to react,' said Melissa. 'Marty got into serious trouble. Don't you ever throw eggs, Jaydene.'

'Oh I won't, don't worry. I wouldn't dare,' she said, her eyes round.

I felt almost as big as Mighty Mart. *I* dared.

'I don't think you need to fight back, Jaydene,' said Melissa. 'If I were you I'd just laugh when Katie and Ingrid say mean things. Act like you don't care. *I* laugh at Chantelle and Laura, or I say, ever so gently, "What's your problem?" and it just totally fazes them.'

'*Really*?' said Jaydene.

'Until the next time,' I said.

Then there was a knock on the door. It was Jaydene's mum, ready to collect her. Her visit was *over*.

Well, nearly. Mum made Jaydene's mum a cup of tea, and then she took her upstairs to see her new sewing room and our new bedroom. Jaydene's mum *loved* all Mum's dresses twirling on hangers all round the room.

'You're so *clever*, Mrs Michaels,' she said. 'These dresses are absolutely beautiful.'

I raised my eyebrows at Jaydene.

It looked like she might be in serious danger of ending up in a cringe-making crinoline herself.

'Come and see Marty and Melissa's bedroom, Mum,' she said quickly.

Jaydene's mum went totally *ecstatic*! She oohed and aahed over the duvet covers and the cushions and the chandelier, but she especially adored the shelf unit.

'Did you get a special carpenter, Mrs Michaels?' she asked.

'No, my husband did it,' said Mum.

'Really! Oh, Mr Michaels, *you're* so clever,' said Jaydene's mum.

When Jaydene left with her mum, all three members of my family spent the next twenty minutes going on and on about her, saying how much they liked her.

'I'm so happy you've got a special best friend at last, Martina,' said Mum, putting her arm round me and giving me a squeeze.

I supposed I was happy too – but Jaydene didn't really seem like *my* best friend any more. She seemed to be *Melissa's* best friend forever. Maybe *that's* the worst thing about my sister. Everyone likes her *best*.

The next Friday Melissa had *her* best friends to tea, to show off our new bedroom. She said she couldn't choose who she liked best so she invited *three* girls – Ali, Nina and Amaleena.

'That's not fair,' I protested. 'I only had *one* friend to tea.'

'You've only *got* one friend,' said Melissa scornfully.

'I've got *heaps* of friends,' I said. 'Micky West and me play together every single lunch time now.'

'You can't ask a *boy* to play in your bedroom,' said Melissa. 'Anyway, he wouldn't be interested in stuff like colour schemes and shelf units.'

'Well, I'm not interested either.'

'That's perfectly obvious. Now listen, I want you to tidy up before Ali and Nina and Amaleena come. I'm sick of you leaving your socks and knickers in a nasty heap on the carpet. Why can't you put them in the clothes basket?'

'Do you know, you sound just like Mum?' I said.

'And take down that silly Mighty Mart poster – it looks awful. I don't want childish scribbles messing up the place.'

'That's *my* bit of corkboard, Dad *said*.'

'Yes, all right, but put something *normal* up – the sort of thing girls your age like – puppies or kittens.' Melissa was talking like she was grown up herself, not just two and a half years older than me. 'And for goodness' sake hide all your tatty old animals.'

Wilma still swam in my bunk bed, but I hadn't been able to stop Jumper jumping out of his kennel, Basil needed to stretch and slither, Polly wanted to give her cramped wings a good flap all round the room, and poor Half-Percy was delicate and needed special loving care in the daylight.

I opened my mouth to explain all this to Melissa, but she didn't even listen.

'Put them in the cupboard!' she said. 'Or else you'll be very, very sorry.'

That really got my back up. Who was Melissa to start giving me orders? She was only my boring, bossy sister. I didn't have to do what *she* said, did I? I *pretended* to tidy everything away on Thursday night. Well, I really did put all my underwear in the clothes basket, and I took down my best Mighty Mart poster, and I hid Wilma under my new slippery duvet, and caged every poor animal in the shelf-unit cupboard overnight.

I *might* just have left them there if Melissa had been really truly grateful, but she barely said thank you.

'I don't believe it!' she said, rolling her eyes. 'Wonders will never cease!'

That's not true gratitude, is it? So on Friday morning after breakfast, when we were going out of the front door, I pretended I needed the toilet urgently. I charged upstairs into the bathroom, grabbed half a dozen items from the dirty clothes basket, rushed into our room and sprinkled them on the floor, opened the cupboard and let my animals loose, and then pinned dear Mighty Mart back in place where she belonged. I searched for a pen. As always, I couldn't find one. I seized a lipstick instead and gave Mighty Mart a speech bubble:

I HATE BOSSY BIG SISTERS WITH BIG FAT BOTTOMS!

'Come *on*, Martina, we'll be late for school,' Mum called.

'Coming!' I said, and skipped downstairs.

Melissa and Mum were none the wiser. I could hardly contain myself on the way to school. I told Jaydene about the fantastic trick I'd played, but she didn't laugh. She looked like she was going to burst into tears.

'Oh, Marty, Melissa will be so upset. She'll want the bedroom to look lovely for all her friends,' she said, agonized.

'Well, it *does* look lovely – *my* sort of lovely, with all my things around to make it my bedroom,' I said.

'Promise you won't get cross with me, Marty, but your things *are* a bit messy,' said Jaydene. 'Poor Melissa.'

'Poor *me*, with no Marty Den any more,' I said.

I told Micky West and all his mates about my bedroom trick while we were playing baseball at lunch time. *They* all thought it was funny. Micky laughed so much he practically fell over.

'You are *funny*, Farty Marty,' he said. '*My* big sister's always nagging at me. I couldn't stand it if I had to share a room with her.'

Oh, I *do* like Micky West. He made me feel all happy and bouncy again – but I started to worry a bit on the way home. Melissa was going on and on about our bedroom to Ali and Nina and Amaleena.

'Just wait till you see it! I chose the colour scheme all myself. And it looks totally cool, like it's a real teenage room,' she boasted, beaming.

She seemed so happy my tummy

started to go tight. Maybe Jaydene was right. Perhaps my trick wasn't funny at all. I started to wish I hadn't done it. I tried to summon up my own superpowers. I thought of Jumper and Basil and Polly and Half-Percy and all my ponies, and *willed* them to pick themselves up and scamper back into the cupboard. I told my socks to hop around the room and then jump into the laundry basket. I made Mighty Mart scrub her lipstick message from her mouth. I willed this so fiercely that Mum wondered why I was pulling funny faces.

'What's the matter, Martina?' she whispered in my ear.

'Nothing, Mum.'

Mum didn't look convinced. 'Are you in trouble at school again?'

'No!'

'Are you sure? Don't fib to me, young lady.'

'I *promise* I'm not in trouble at school,' I said.

I *wasn't* in trouble at school. But I was going to be in trouble at home. Big-time.

I tried to charge upstairs when Mum opened the front door. I wanted to whirl round the bedroom putting everything to rights before Melissa and her boring friends set foot in it – but Mum caught hold of me.

'No, you stay down in the kitchen with me. Let Melissa show the girls her bedroom in peace. She let you have a private time with Jaydene when you first came home from school.'

'But, Mum, I just —'

'No! You can help me fix a little snack for everyone. You do as you're told!'

I couldn't even take refuge with Dad because he was seeing a client in his office. I was forced to follow Mum into the kitchen. I heard a whole lot of squealing from upstairs.

'It sounds as if they like the bedroom!' Mum said happily.

My ears were sharper than hers. I'd heard Melissa squealing too. I knew I was for it.

My heart hammered in my chest as I stood in the kitchen, mechanically arranging chocolate biscuits on a plate, while Mum poured five smoothies into our fancy glasses.

'There now,' she said, putting them all on a tray. She looked at me. 'What *is* it, Martina? You've barely said a word since you got out of school.

'I'm fine,' I said in a tiny voice.

'Are you feeling a bit left out of things? Look, tell you what. *You* carry the tray upstairs to the girls.'

'But – but I might drop it,' I said.

'Well, carry it *carefully*. I haven't filled

the glasses very full so they won't spill. Just take your time.'

I certainly did that. I went up the stairs in slow motion. My ears waggled like bats, straining to hear what they were saying. I decided I might just say sorry to Melissa. Nothing elaborate, just: 'Sorry I made the room a bit messy.'

I could clear it up in a trice. Gather my animals, kick my socks under the beds and slip the poster off the board. The room would be back to rights in five seconds. I could do it all as if I really had superpowers, whirling round, and they'd all laugh at me and pat me on my curly head and wish they had a funny little sister just like me.

They were laughing *already*. I put down the tray and opened the bedroom door. Ali and Nina and Amaleena were sitting on the bottom bunk. My socks were already kicked underneath. My Mighty Mart poster was torn down and ripped in half!

Melissa was sitting on the floor in the

midst of my animals. 'Honestly, she is so *pathetic*,' she was saying. 'I think she's seriously retarded. She acts just like a two-year-old. She thinks this ridiculous object' – she seized Basil and waggled him – 'is a snake! A snake, I ask you. Anyone can see it's just my mum's old tights.'

Ali and Nina and Amaleena all burst out laughing. Basil hung his head. His sewn eyes looked at me imploringly.

'Stop it!' I said, bursting into the room.

Melissa whirled Basil round and round, making him feel terribly sick and giddy.

'Give me Basil!' I shrieked.

'He's not Basil, he's just old tights, stupid,' said Melissa, dangling him right in my face. Suddenly he really *looked* like Mum's old tights. His face was mortified.

Melissa dropped him on the carpet disdainfully and then picked up poor little Half-Percy. 'And look at *this* mangled bit of fluff!' she said, tossing him in the air like a ball. 'You'll never guess what. Marty stuck the head to one of my hairbrushes and said it was a *porcupine*!'

Ali and Nina and Amaleena all rocked with laughter, clutching each other.

'Look at this,' Melissa carried on relentlessly, picking up Polly. Her poor head flopped down and one wing was crumpled. 'She just cut it out from the back of a cornflake packet, she says it's a real parrot and makes it fly – *flap flap flap*!' She steered poor Polly through thin air in a terrible mockery of flying. 'Hang on – it looks dead to me,' she said, and she turned Polly upside down, claws in the air.

'*You'll* be dead in a minute,' I said, springing at her.

'Oh help!' said Melissa, pretending to be frightened. She put her hand on my chest, shoving hard, holding me off. 'It's Mighty Mart come to squash me flat with her superpowers!'

Ali and Nina and Amaleena practically wet themselves. I lost my footing on the rug and sat down abruptly.

'Oh dear, have you bumped *your* big fat bottom?' said Melissa.

'You shut up, you pig!' I said.

'Oh, lickle crybaby,' said Melissa.

I *wasn't* crying. My eyes were simply watering with shock.

'You are such a baby, Marty.'

Something flashed inside my head. I rolled over, jumped up, and ran over to the bunk beds. Ali and Nina and Amaleena all ducked, as if they thought I was attacking them. I snatched up Melissa's pillow and grabbed Baba from her shadowy hidey-hole.

'*You're* the baby!' I said. 'You make out you're so grown up yet you can't get to sleep without your tatty old baby doll!' I held Baba by the legs, swinging her about.

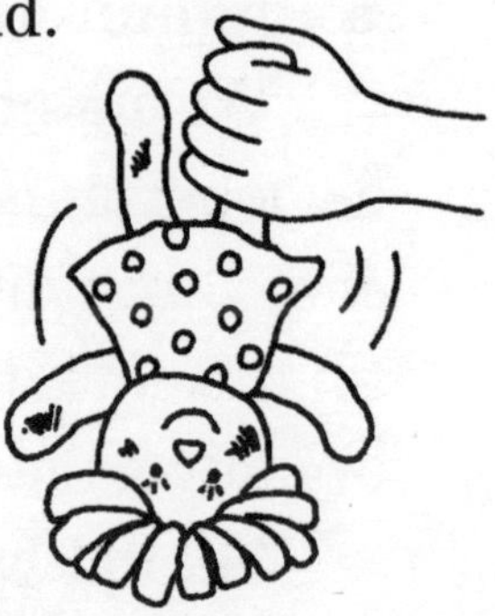

Ali and Nina and Amaleena all gawped.

'She's – she's not mine!' said Melissa, but she'd gone *scarlet*, as if she'd smeared her precious lipstick all over her face. It was obvious she was fibbing.

Ali and Nina and Amaleena all tittered uncomfortably.

I barked a triumphant hyena laugh. 'There! Who's a baby now?' I said, twirling Baba around.

Then Baba suddenly became a whole lot

lighter. Most of her dropped onto the carpet and sprawled there. I was left holding one of her old withered legs.

'Oh!' I said, stricken. 'Oh, Melissa, I'm sorry. I didn't mean to break her.'

We all stared at Melissa. For a moment it looked as if she was going to cry. I could see her chin wobbling. But then she laughed shakily. She nudged the remains of Baba with her toe.

'As if I care about that old thing,' she said, and she kicked her under the bunk amongst my dirty socks.

'Hey, have you seen my Justin Bieber photo?' she went on, grabbing it and thrusting it at them.

Ali and Nina and Amaleena all squealed excitedly, distracted. I gave them the forgotten tray of smoothies and biscuits and crept away.

Mum found me hunched up on the stairs. 'Oh dear.

You look a poor lost soul. Well, you can't play with Dad because he's still seeing his client. I think she's a total time-waster. I bet she just takes an armful of brochures away and never comes back. How about you coming and fixing the supper with me, Martina? I'm making a trifle. You can lick out the bowl.'

Mum was trying to be so nice to me, and somehow it made me feel much worse. After Dad's client had gone at last, he read me a story. Doing different funny voices. I huddled up beside him and tried to laugh in all the right places. Dad was being even nicer than Mum, and that made me feel worse of all. The moment Ali and Nina and Amaleena went home I was sure Melissa would tell on me – and then I'd be for it.

I was right.

When they were all gone, Mum turned to Melissa and gave her a big hug. 'Did you have a lovely time with your friends, darling? I bet they loved your new bedroom!' she said.

Melissa glared at me.

'Don't tell, don't tell, don't tell!' I mouthed at her.

But Melissa always told.

'No, I *didn't* have a lovely time! Marty totally humiliated me. She deliberately made a huge mess and threw all her stupid animals about, and wrote that I had a big bottom in lipstick! I just about died,' she said.

'*What*?'

I tried to make Mum understand, but I couldn't get the words out properly. I appealed to Dad, but he seemed horrified too.

'I just can't believe you could be so mean and spiteful, Martina,' he said. 'Especially when Melissa tried so hard to make your friend Jaydene welcome. I'm thoroughly ashamed of you.'

I was sent up to bed early in disgrace. Mum and Dad barely said goodnight to me when Melissa came up to bed. Melissa wasn't speaking to me either.

'I'm sorry I amputated Baba,' I whispered into the darkness.

Melissa didn't answer. She waited for a few minutes after Mum and Dad had switched off the light and gone downstairs. Then she got out of her bunk bed and crept over to the bedroom door.

'Where are you going, Melissa?' I whispered.

She took no notice. She stole out. I lay there miserably, wrapped tight in Wilma, wondering if she was going downstairs to tell about Baba too – but after a minute she came tiptoeing back. She'd been in the sewing room. I heard her get back into bed and saw the glow of her torch. I hung down over the edge of my top bunk, bumping my head on the ladder, and saw that Melissa was sitting up in bed, sewing Baba's leg back on.

'Oh, Melissa, is she OK again now? I said I'm really sorry,' I said.

'You *will* be sorry. Very, very, very sorry,' Melissa said ominously.

She didn't say anything else at all, even though I begged her to talk to me. When Baba had two legs again, she snapped off her torch and lay down. After a few minutes I heard her breathing heavily, fast asleep.

I couldn't get to sleep for *ages*.

The next morning I was so tired I couldn't wake up properly. I was dimly aware of Melissa rustling around the room very early, long before Mum and Dad were up, and I wondered what she was doing – but then I fell asleep again. Later on I heard Mum calling me to get up, but I turned over and buried my head under my pillow. I lay there, hearing the clank and clatter of the recycling lorry as it chugged its way slowly along the road, and as the great roar faded away, I dozed again.

'Marty! Mum says you've *got* to come down for breakfast now,' said Melissa, putting her head round our bedroom door. There was something odd about her voice.

I sat up in bed. 'What is it? What's up?' My heart started thudding. 'What have you *done*?'

'You'll find out,' said Melissa ominously, and sauntered off to the bathroom.

I clambered down my bunk-bed ladder and looked around the room. My shelf was empty. No Jumper or Basil or Polly or Half-Percy. Even Patches and Gee-Up and Sugarlump and Merrylegs and Dandelion and Starlight were missing. I ran to my cupboard and pulled it open. It was empty!

I tried Melissa's cupboard but that was just neatly stacked with her own stuff. I looked in the wardrobe, in Melissa's dressing-table drawers – I even looked in her jewellery box. I looked everywhere.

My animals were missing.

You'll be very, very, very sorry!

Melissa had stolen my poor dear pets! What had she done with them? Had she dumped them in the rubbish bin as she'd often threatened?

I ran downstairs in my pyjamas, hurtled across the hall and out of the front door. I charged over to the wheelie bin in my bare feet, pulled up the lid – and saw it was *empty*. The recycling lorry had already been. I thought of my poor animals caught up in the gigantic steel maw of that great recycling monster. I knew what would happen next. I'd seen the end of *Toy Story 3*.

I started running down our garden path, yelling, though the recycling lorry wasn't even in sight now.

'Martina! What on earth are you playing at? You are *so* going to drive me crazy! Get back into the house this *instant*!' Mum shouted, running after me and grabbing me.

'But, Mum, you don't understand! My *animals*!' I screamed.

The nosy old lady next door opened her window and leaned out. 'My goodness, what's all that noise? What's the matter with Martina?'

'Nothing! She's perfectly fine!' Mum called, in a high strangled voice. She pulled me closer and hissed in my face, 'Get back in the house right this second and stop shaming me!' She dragged me back indoors, struggling and kicking.

'What are you playing at now, Marty?' Dad called from the kitchen. 'Are you *crying*?'

'I'll give her something to cry about in a minute!' said Mum. 'Now go upstairs and get washed and dressed *immediately*. And what's that smell? Oh no, it's the toast burning.'

Mum and Dad went into the kitchen, bickering about the burned toast. I looked up the stairs – and there was Melissa hanging over the banisters, grinning down at me.

'Oh dear, have the dustbin men come already?' she said.

I shot up the stairs like a rocket, my fists clenched. Melissa flew into our bedroom and tried to slam the door shut on me, but I hurled myself against it and forced it open.

'You pig, you hateful wicked pig, you've stolen all my animals!' I yelled, pummelling her.

She ducked away from me, laughing.

'I *told* you you'd be very, very, sorry,' she said, insufferably smug. 'You brought it all on yourself, making all that mess and then pulling Baba to bits.'

Baba! I ran to Melissa's bunk, felt under her pillow and pulled Baba out. Right! If I'd lost all my dear precious animals, then Melissa was going to lose her stupid baby.

'Give me Baba!' she said, suddenly worried.

I was much too quick for her. I ran up my bunk-bed ladder like a monkey and flopped down on my top bunk, tearing at Baba with my bare hands. Her newly sewn leg came off at once, *and* the other one, and – grisly triumph – her whole head came off with one gigantic tug.

'Baba!' Melissa screamed, and started climbing the ladder to rescue her.

'Get away! Get off!' I said, kicking out with

my feet, determined to tear Baba to bits first. I kicked again as hard as I could – and the whole ladder jerked sideways, the little hooks on the end becoming detached. Melissa screamed again and lost her grip on the rungs. She seemed suspended in the air in the weirdest slow motion, her mouth gaping – and then she fell to the floor with a terrible thump.

I sat still on the top bunk, staring down at her, pieces of Baba in my hands. Melissa lay very still too, on her back, her head tilted sideways.

'Melissa?' I said croakily.

Melissa didn't reply.

I swallowed. 'Please, Melissa. You are all right, aren't you?' I whispered.

I dropped Baba and then swung myself carefully over the side of the bunk beds, ignoring the shaky ladder. I knelt beside Melissa. Her eyes were shut, her mouth still a little open. I couldn't see any blood anywhere. She just looked as if she were asleep.

'Melissa, wake up!' I said. I reached out and gave her a little shake. 'Stop it, you're frightening me. I know you're only playing. Open your eyes!'

She took no notice. I tickled her under her chin. Melissa is terribly ticklish and always hunches her shoulders and squeals if you tickle her neck. She didn't even twitch.

'Oh, Melissa!' I said. And then I shouted at the top of my voice: '*Mum! Dad! Come quick!*'

'What is it *now*? And what was that terrible thump? I'm warning you, Martina, I've had just about enough of your silly tricks,' Mum called as she ran up the stairs – but then she gasped as she came into our room. She threw herself down on the carpet beside Melissa, and bent over her head.

'Oh my God!' she whispered.

Dad came running too. He took one look at Melissa, and then ran back down to the phone in the hall.

'Yes, Ambulance, please. It's an emergency. My daughter's had a serious fall. Can you get an ambulance to 99 Milner Drive as soon as possible?'

I crouched in a corner, trembling. This was it. I'd done some terrible things in my time, but this was the worst one ever. I'd killed my sister.

Mum and Dad knelt on either side of Melissa, holding her hands and whispering to her. I kept waiting for them to look over at me and ask me about the accident. And then what would they do? They would probably hate me for ever, and I wouldn't blame them. I hated me too. Would they tell the police on me? Would I get tried for murder and sent to prison? But I hadn't *meant* to murder her, had I? I looked down at my hands. They were still clutching Baba's face and one leg. I dropped them, shuddering.

Then the ambulance people came. They listened to Melissa's chest and felt her very gently, and then put her in a neck brace and slipped her onto a stretcher.

'Is she really dead?' I whispered, but they didn't even hear me.

They said Mum could go with Melissa in the ambulance and Dad would have to follow in his car.

'Right, Marty. Come on,' he said. He saw my bare feet. 'Put your boots on. Quick.'

I shoved my feet into my Converse boots and followed him. 'I'm frightened of hospitals,' I mumbled.

'So am I,' said Dad. 'But we've got to get there to be with Melissa.'

'Dad – Dad, Melissa looked *dead,*' I said.

'Stop it,' he said. 'She'll – she'll be all right. I'm sure she will be. She's unconscious because she's had a bump on her head. Did she fall off the ladder? I can't *believe* I didn't fix it more securely.'

'It wasn't your fault, Dad,' I said. I wasn't quite brave enough to say it was all *my* fault. I kept trying to make my mouth say it. I opened my lips but no sound came out.

When we got to the hospital, we had to drive round and round the car park to find a space. Then we ran round and round all the red-brick buildings, trying to find out where

they'd taken Melissa. At last we found the right reception area at A & E. Melissa was supposed to be in a cubicle at the end, but when we pulled the curtain back there was no sign of her. Dad and I clutched each other's hands, staring at the empty bed.

'Oh, Dad, they've taken her away! She *must* be dead,' I said, starting to sob.

'No, no, they'll be testing her or X-raying her – something like that,' said Dad, but the palm of his hand was clammy with sweat.

He went to ask where she was now, while I sat on the end of the bed with my eyes tight shut, making all sorts of vows inside my head. I promised I'd never ever fight with Melissa again, just so long as she got better. I still felt a terrible pang at the thought of my poor animals. I couldn't quite forgive Melissa for doing such a dreadful thing – but I didn't want her *dead*.

'It's OK, Curlynob,' said Dad, coming back into the cubicle. 'I was right – they've taken her off for some sort of scan. We'll go and try and find her. OK?'

We walked down miles of corridors, following red routes and green routes and going upstairs and round corners. At long long last we found Mum, leaning against the wall, her face greenish-white, tears running down her cheeks.

'Oh, Mum, is she dead?' I cried.

'No, no, darling. Come here.' Mum held out her arms and gave me a big hug.

I clung to her. Mum rocked me as if I were a little baby. It made me cry harder because I was sure she'd thrust me away from her if she knew what I'd done.

'Melissa's having her head scanned at the moment, just to make sure she's all right, but she's already woken up, and that's obviously a very good sign,' said Mum.

'She's really conscious?' said Dad, joining in the hug.

'Well, she's still a bit woozy, and they want to keep her as quiet as possible at the moment – but her eyes are open and she's taking everything in.'

Then Melissa herself was wheeled back on a trolley. She was still lying down and she looked very pale and floppy, but her eyes really *were* open.

'Oh, Melissa!' said Dad, and for the second time in my life I saw him cry. 'Is she really all right?' he asked the nurse.

'As far as we can tell, she's fine,' said the nurse. 'But just to be on the safe side we'll put her in the children's ward overnight so we can keep an eye on her.'

'Can I stay with her?' Mum asked.

'Yes, of course you can,' said the nurse.

She nodded at me. 'You can come back and see your sister again at visiting time, Pyjama Queen.'

'What?'

Mum suddenly gasped. 'Oh, for heaven's sake, Martina, you're still in your pyjamas! What are you two like?'

She told Dad and me off, but fondly. Melissa said nothing, but she smiled at me. I wanted to give her a great big hug, but she still looked too scary lying there, as limp as poor Baba.

Dad took me back to the car park, anxiously trying to shield me in case people stared at me in my pyjamas.

When we got back home, he clapped the palm of his hand to his forehead. 'Oh no, I've just remembered – I've got a client coming to discuss cruise options. I suppose I'd better still see her. You go and get washed and dressed, Marty, and then play quietly in your room,' he said.

I made myself scarce upstairs. I couldn't bear to see the ladder lying drunkenly sideways, so I hauled it up and managed to hook it back in place.

I felt so bad in the overwhelmingly empty room that I grabbed Wilma and dived under the bunk beds in the dark, right up against the wall. Something slithered against me, something pecked my toe, something nuzzled into me. I gasped, feeling around frantically. All my animals were hiding underneath! Even Jumper was there, though he'd been squashed up uncomfortably with his head under his paws. Melissa *hadn't* put them out in the rubbish bin! She'd just hidden them away to teach me a lesson, and here they were, safe and sound . . . while poor Baba was in bits and Melissa was lying in hospital.

I rescued all my animals and laid them out neatly on my top bunk with Wilma to recover. Then I searched around, gathering up the bits of Baba. I went into Mum's

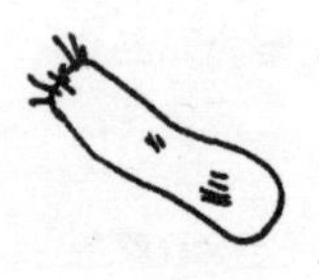

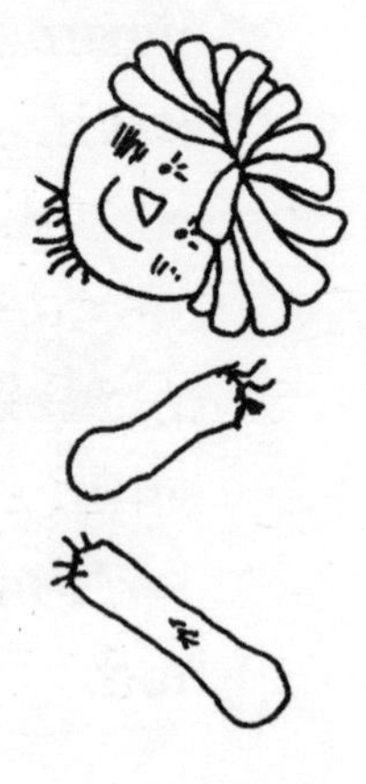

sewing room, shuddering at all the fancy dresses and costumes hanging from the rail in plastic bags, and helped myself to a needle and cotton. Then I sat down in my bedroom and started the

long, slow, laborious process of putting Baba together again.

I wasn't good at sewing like Melissa. I'd only ever sewn the edge of the black bear cushion. I sat down on him and he growled encouragement. My stitches were terribly big at first, and Baba's head wobbled horribly even when it was sewn back in place. I had to pull all the stitches out and start all over again. This time I managed tiny little mouse stitches, and at last Baba's head sat firmly on her neck.

Dad's client took ages and then walked off saying she would think everything over. Dad came up to see what I was doing, sighing – and was taken aback to see me sewing Baba.

'Oh, Marty, you're a little treasure!' he said. 'You're sewing old Baba up to take to Melissa in hospital! I wish your mum could see you now. You're *such* a good girl!'

'I'm not, Dad. I'm bad. I'm very, very bad,' I said miserably. I tried to tell him, but I still couldn't get the words past my lips. I went a little weepy again, worrying about Melissa. 'Dad, do you think Melissa really *is* going to get completely better, right as rain?'

'Yes, I'm sure she will. Look, you're not meant to phone people in hospital, but I'll text Mum just to check.'

How's M? he texted.

Mum texted back, Looking much better!

I started sewing Baba's leg back, and Dad went to answer the door again. It was Jaydene's mum! She was very concerned when Dad told her that Melissa was in hospital, but then asked if she could have a word with him 'in a professional capacity'.

I thought she was wanting him to book a holiday for her. She certainly stayed huddled in his office for ages. I sewed Baba until she was as good as new (well, almost), and then I held her tight, cradling her, telling her I'd take her to see Melissa this very afternoon.

After Dad had shown Jaydene's mum out of the front door, he came bounding up the stairs to me. 'Guess what!' he said.

'Jaydene's mum's booked a holiday?'

'No. Better than that!'

'She wants Mum to make one of her frilly dresses?' I said. 'Oh, *poor* Jaydene.'

'No, no, she doesn't want Mum to work for her. She wants *me*! She took a shine to your shelf units and wants me to do something similar in Jaydene's bedroom. I explained that I'm not a proper carpenter or anything, but she seems to think I'm the bee's knees. She asked how much it would cost and I suggested what's actually quite a cheeky sum, but she seems very happy

with it. Oh, Marty, what a turn-up! Mum will be so pleased.'

'Can you text Mum again, just to see if Melissa is still all right?' I asked.

So Dad texted: Melissa? and Mum texted back: Wide awake and talking!

Dad gave me a happy hug. I felt very happy too that Melissa really did sound better – and very scared in case she was talking about *me*, telling Mum that I'd kicked her off the ladder.

Dad made us beans on toast for lunch, usually one of my favourites, but I was so anxious it was a struggle to get it all down. Then we set off for hospital again. I had Baba carefully wrapped up in a little blanket to give to Melissa. She had a head and all four limbs again, though she still looked a bit limp and seedy. I felt limp and seedy too. I hoped I wasn't going to sick up the baked beans straight away. I held a long conversation with

Mighty Mart in my head, wanting her to use her superpowers to make Melissa absolutely one hundred per cent better – apart from one teeny tiny memory lapse so she couldn't remember a thing about this morning.

It took us even longer to find a space in the hospital car park as so many more people were arriving for the two o'clock visiting time. Then we had another long trek down blue routes and yellow routes, this time to find the children's wing of the hospital.

There was a long corridor to the children's ward. Most of it was just dingy cream and brown paint – but one section at the end was painted like bright blue sky with white fluffy clouds and a rainbow. A girl with short spiky hair, wearing very stained jeans, was up a ladder painting a flock of bright green birds.

'Oh, wow!' I said, suddenly distracted. 'I didn't know you were allowed to paint on *walls*!'

'Don't you dare try it at home, Marty,' said Dad.

The girl grinned at me from her ladder. 'It's fun,' she said.

'I've never seen *green* birds,' I said. 'They're really cool.'

'They're parakeets – but I might paint all different-coloured birds just for the fun of it. Pink birds, orange birds, purple birds. Multi-coloured birds.'

'Tartan birds, like my boots!' I said.

'Don't be silly, Marty!' Dad sighed, but the girl looked pleased.

'Great idea,' she said.

'Oh, our Marty's full of those,' said Dad. 'Come on now, let's find Melissa.'

My tummy started churning again. We went through the swing doors into the ward and peered along the rows of beds. I looked for a pale face and a limp body lying under sheets. I was astonished to spot Melissa down at the end, propped up on pillows, pink-cheeked and smiling.

'Oh, Melissa!' I said, and I ran headlong down the ward and threw my arms round her.

'Careful, careful, Martina, she's still a bit fragile!' said Mum, but she didn't sound cross.

'Oh, Melissa, you really *are* better!' I said, hugging her hard.

'Yes, I'm fine now, Marty! You're squashing me!' said Melissa. She felt for the blanket. 'What's that?'

'I brought you Baba,' I said, making her head peep out of the blanket. 'I sewed her all up again. I'm so sorry,' I whispered.

'She doesn't want that awful grubby old thing in hospital,' said Mum.

'Yes I do,' said Melissa, taking Baba, still wrapped in the blanket, and tucking her down under the sheet.

'I'm so pleased you're looking perky again, sweetheart,' said Dad, giving Melissa a hug too. 'You gave us such a fright. I'm going to fix that ladder so it can't possibly slip again.'

'Yes, how exactly did it happen, Melissa?' Mum asked, holding her hand.

I swallowed. Melissa looked at Mum. She looked at Dad. She looked at me, long and hard. She remembered all right. There was a roaring in my ears as I waited for her answer. The baked beans bubbled in my tummy. This was it. Melissa always always told on me. She was going to tell on me now, and Mum and Dad would hate me for ever.

Melissa was still looking me straight in the eye. She saw my look of agony. She hesitated. Then gave me a very tiny wink.

'I don't really know what happened. I just slipped,' she said.

'But why were you going up the ladder in the first place?' said Mum. 'It's Martina's bunk on top.'

'Oh, we were just playing,' said Melissa. 'Mum, I feel so much better. I haven't got a headache. I don't feel sick. Can't I just go home now?'

She chatted away to Mum and Dad while I sat there in a daze. She hadn't told on me! Melissa might not feel sick now, but *I* did. Not just sick with relief. *Really* sick.

'Mum, I need the toilet,' I said urgently.

'It's along the corridor, halfway down,' said Mum. 'Shall I take you?'

'I'll find it,' I mumbled, and hurtled off. I didn't even have time to nod to the girl up the ladder. I shot into the Ladies in the nick of time and threw up. I did it very neatly down the toilet, and then I rinsed my mouth out at the basin. I stared at myself in the mirror. It was all right! Melissa was better – and she hadn't told on me! She didn't want to get me into trouble. Oh, I loved loved *loved* my sister so much!

I did a little dance of joy as I came out of the Ladies. The girl up the ladder laughed at me.

'They are seriously cool boots,' she said. She beckoned to me. 'Come and look.'

I ran up to her and saw she'd painted a little bird with red and yellow checks, *exactly* like my Converse boots.

'Oh, I *love* it!' I said.

'It was your idea, not mine,' she said. 'What else shall I paint? I want to make it a really bright happy picture with heaps of things for children to look at.'

I stared at the blue sky. 'You could paint Batman and Superman and Spider Man all swooping about the sky,' I suggested.

'Excellent!' she said.

'And – and maybe Mighty Mart?' I added breathlessly.

'Who's Mighty Mart?'

'She's my own superhero,' I said. 'I made her up. I do lots of comics about her.'

'Brilliant! What does she look like, then?'

'Well . . . a bit like me, but she's much older and she's much taller too, and she's got big arms to bash all the bad people and long legs so that she can leap right up into the sky,' I said, demonstrating.

'You draw her for me,' said the girl, offering me a pencil.

'On the *wall*?' I asked. My hand hovered in the air. I *so* wanted to. 'But what if I mess it up? I'm quite good at drawing, but not as good as you.'

'Why not give it a go? You could do it very lightly, so that if you don't like it, I could always paint right over it, easy-peasy. Go on, give it a go, Marty.'

'How do you know my name?'

'I heard your dad calling you. My name's Mattie – almost the same.'

I took the pencil and started drawing very, very lightly on the wall, holding my breath. But Mighty Mart sprang straight out of the pencil tip the way she always did. I knew her so well, my line didn't wobble once.

'Looking good,' said Mattie. She scratched her spiky hair.

'Whoops! You've got a bit of blue paint in your hair now,' I said.

'Oh well, I'll just kid on it's wacky hair dye,' said Mattie. 'Hey, Marty, that's really *good*. Mighty Mart is flying high!'

'Maybe I could do a Mighty Matt too,' I said. 'Is your name really Mattie?'

'No, it's Matilda, but I hate it. No one calls me that, except my mum when she's cross with me.'

'I'm Martina. *My* mum calls me that all the time – though actually she's often cross with me too. I can't believe this. You're like my twin sister, but bigger. Oh! I'd better get back to my *real* sister,' I said.

Just then Dad came out into the corridor. '*There* you are, Marty! I should have guessed,' he said.

'She's been helping me,' said Mattie. 'Maybe she can come and help again when you're visiting her sister?'

'I think she'll be going home tomorrow,' said Dad.

'Oh!' I said, drooping. I almost hoped that Melissa would have a little relapse. *Almost* – but not really.

'Well, never mind, Marty. I'm hoping to be around town quite a lot, painting

murals,' said Mattie. 'I left art college last year but I've never sold a single painting, so I'm giving this a go instead. I'm trying to get established. I'm doing this for the hospital for nothing. It's hard setting up your own business nowadays.'

'Tell me about it!' said Dad.

He liked Mattie a lot too. He told her all about his travel service and how it hadn't really worked, but maybe now he'd start up as a carpenter designing shelf units. He told her about Mum and her new dressmaking career too.

I didn't join in much. I was too busy concentrating. Mattie had lent me her paintbrush and I was ever so, ever so carefully painting in Mighty Mart's orange cape and blue tunic and red tights and tartan Converse boots. These

were particularly tricky, but I didn't go over the lines *once*.

'For heaven's sake!' said Mum, coming out into the corridor too. 'I thought you'd both got lost. What are you *doing*, Martina?'

'She's helping me with my mural,' said Mattie. 'Oh wow, Marty, she looks absolutely wonderful!'

We stared at Mighty Mart in all her carefully coloured glory.

'It's Mighty Mart!' said Dad, laughing. 'She looks great, Marty!'

Mum walked right up to the wall, having a closer look. 'Did you really paint her all yourself, Martina?' she asked.

I nodded proudly.

'Well, it's very good,' she said. 'Very, very good. No scribbles, no smudges – it looks almost professional! Though why you always have to draw that silly comic character beats me.'

'I love Mighty Mart,' said Mattie. She fished in the back pocket of her jeans and found a card. 'There – it's got my phone number and email. I just thought – maybe I could run some art workshops for kids in the holidays? Maybe Marty would like to come along?'

Maybe?!

We went back to see Melissa and I talked non-stop about my new friend, Mattie, and my brilliant new mural-painting career.

Melissa rolled her eyes. 'You must absolutely promise not to paint on *our* walls, Marty,' she said. 'If I find even the tiniest *speck* of Mighty Mart anywhere, you'll be very, very sorry.'

'I won't, I promise,' I said. I looked her straight in the eye. 'I owe you big-time,

Melissa. I'm going to keep our bedroom extra-tidy now, and I'll put all my clothes away and keep my animals in the cupboard. I'm going to be the best sister ever, Melissa, you'll see.'

Melissa and Mum and Dad all laughed at me – but I really meant it. When I went to bed that night, I put my socks and knickers in the laundry basket, and kissed Jumper and Basil and Polly and Half-Percy goodnight and tucked them up comfortably in the cupboard. I laid Patches and Gee-Up and Sugarlump and Merrylegs and Dandelion and Starlight down to sleep on their shelf, making them all lie neatly the same way. I made a supreme effort even though Melissa wasn't there to notice.

Dad fixed the bunk-bed ladder so it couldn't slip any more.

'But you must still be very, very careful, Martina,' said Mum. 'I think the sooner we can afford proper twin beds the better!'

She and Dad kissed me goodnight. Dad said, 'Night-night, sleep tight, don't let the bugs bite.'

I couldn't sleep tight for ages. I wound Wilma right round me, but somehow she wasn't quite company enough. It felt so quiet and still in the big bedroom by myself. I knew Melissa was going to be all right. Mum was collecting her from hospital in the morning. But I still worried even so. It felt so odd being without her. I wanted to whisper and giggle and play around with her. We might fight all the time – but it was *fun*. I couldn't wait for her to come home again.

I snuffled mournfully, missing her sweet rose smell. I listened to the silence, wishing I could hear her gentle steady snoring. I missed her so much.

It was wonderful welcoming her home the next day and playing with her in our bedroom. That's the best thing about my sister – she's always *there*. She sticks up for me. She understands about school stuff. She gives me secret cuddles when I need them. And she doesn't tell on me – not when it really, really matters. She's the best sister in the whole world and I love her to bits.

SISTERS

I've always thought it would be wonderful to be part of a very large family. I used to love reading books about big families like *Little Women* and *What Katy Did*. I'd imagine what it would be like to have lots of sisters. I often write rather wistfully about sisters who are very close to each other, like Ruby and Garnet in *Double Act* and Pearl and Jodie in *My Sister Jodie*. I was an only child and I longed for a sister to play with. I used to pretend I had one. I'd mutter to this imaginary person as I played with my dolls and she'd talk back to me. Sometimes we'd even have arguments!

By Jacqueline Wilson

. . . and turn the page for lots more about sisters!

READING NOTES

- In *The Worst Thing About My Sister*, Marty and Melissa are very different! Write a description of both girls and their personalities. Can you spot things that explain why they argue so often? Do you think they would get along better if they were more alike?

- The main character in *The Worst Thing About My Sister* is tomboy Marty, so when the girls fall out, we always hear her side of the story! But do you think girlie Melissa is always to blame for their arguments – or is Marty sometimes in the wrong? Pick out three arguments from the story and try to decide why they started, and how the girls could have acted differently.

- What do you think the hardest thing about having a sister could be? And the nicest thing? If you have a sister, describe your happiest memory of her. If you don't have a sister, you could always write about your best school friend!

- If you could write a letter to Marty and Melissa, what would you say to them to help them get along better? You might have some good advice for them. You could even add some fun ideas for things the girls could do together – like baking, drawing, or putting on a play at home!

Jacqueline Wilson loves writing about sisters in her books – and she loves reading about them too. Some of her favourite books are about sisters. Have you read any of them?

Nancy and Plum

My favourite book when I was a child was *Nancy and Plum* by Betty MacDonald. Nancy and Plum are two orphaned sisters stuck in a children's home run by hateful Mrs Monday. Nancy is a shy, dreamy girl of ten, with long red plaits. Plum is a fierce, funny girl of eight, with short fair plaits. They play all sorts of inventive, imaginary games together and love reading. They decide to run away and eventually find a wonderful new home on a farm with Mr and Mrs Campbell, who give them lots of love and hugs and treats!

Ballet Shoes

I liked *Ballet Shoes* by Noel Streatfeild – about three orphaned sisters this time! Pauline, Petrova and Posy get to go to stage school. Pauline is the pretty one who loves acting. Petrova is plain and hates having to prance about on stage – she wants to fly planes.

Posy is a little show-off who is seriously gifted at ballet. They are such true-to-life, realistic girls. I used to imagine I was at stage school with them and pretended my pink bedroom slippers were ballet shoes!

Little Women

I loved Victorian stories like *Little Women* by Louisa M. Alcott, about four sisters, Meg, Jo, Beth and Amy. I liked Jo best, because she was the most lively, an untidy tomboy who loved reading and writing her own stories.

What Katy Did

I also loved *What Katy Did* by Susan Coolidge. Katy is the oldest and naughtiest child in a very large family, with three sisters – Clover, Elsie and Johnnie – and two brothers too! She also has a kind and cheerful older cousin, Helen, who is almost like another sister. Katy has a fall from a swing and is in bed, unable to walk, for a very long time. She naturally grumbles and complains – but there is a happy ending!

By Jacqueline Wilson

Have you read these other fantastic stories about sisters by Jacqueline Wilson?

Ruby and Garnet are identical twins – but they don't always want the same things . . .

DOUBLE ACT

We're twins. I'm Ruby. She's Garnet.

We're identical. There's very few people who can tell us apart. Well, until we start talking. I tend to go on and on. Garnet is much quieter.

That's because I can't get a word in edgeways.

We are exactly the same height and weight. I eat a bit more than Garnet. I love sweets, and I like salty things too. I once ate thirteen packets of crisps in one day. All salt-and-vinegar flavour. I love lots of salt and vinegar on chips too. Chips are my special weakness. I go munch munch munch gulp and they're gone. So then I have to snaffle some of Garnet's. She doesn't mind.

Yes I do.

I don't get fatter because I charge around more. I hate sitting still. Garnet will hunch up over a book for hours, but I get the fidgets. We're both quite good at running, Garnet and me. At our last sports day at school we beat everyone, even the boys. We came first. Well, I did, actually. Garnet came second. But that's not surprising, seeing as I'm the eldest. We're both ten. But I'm twenty minutes older. I was the bossy baby who pushed out first. Garnet came second.

We live with our dad and our gran.

Dad often can't tell us apart in the morning at breakfast, but then his eyes aren't always

open properly. He just swallows black coffee as he shoves on his clothes and then dashes off for his train. Dad works in an office in London and he hates it. He's always tired out when he gets home. But he can tell us apart by then. It's easier in the evening. My plaits are generally coming undone and my T-shirt's probably stained. Garnet stays as neat as a new pin.

That's what our gran says. Gran always used to have pins stuck all down the front of her cardi. We had to be very careful when we hugged her. Sometimes she even had pins sticking out of her mouth. That was when she did her dressmaking. She used to work in this posh Fashion House, pinning and tucking and sewing all day long. Then, after . . .

Well, Gran had to look after us, you see, so she did dressmaking at home. For private customers. Mostly very large ladies who wanted posh frocks. Garnet and I always got the giggles when we peeped at them in their underwear.

Gran made all our clothes too. That was *awful*. It was bad enough Gran being old-fashioned and making us have our hair in plaits. But our clothes made us a laughing stock at school, though some of the mums said we looked a picture.

We had frilly frocks in summer and dinky pleated skirts in winter, and Gran knitted too – angora boleros that made us itch, and matching jumpers and cardis for the cold. Twinsets. And a right silly set of twins we looked too.

But then Gran's arthritis got worse. She'd always had funny fingers and a bad hip and a naughty knee. But soon she got so she'd screw up her face when she got up or sat down, and her fingers swelled sideways and she couldn't make them work.

She can't do her dressmaking now. It's a shame, because she did like doing it so much. But there's one Amazing Advantage. We get to wear shop clothes now. And because Gran can't really make it on the bus into town, we get to *choose.*

Well. Ruby gets to choose.

I choose for both of us. T-shirts. Leggings. Jeans. Matching ones, of course. We still want to look alike. We just want to look normal.

Only I suppose we're not really like the normal sort of family you read about in books. We read a lot of books. Dad is the worst. He keeps on and on buying them — not just new ones, but heaps of old dusty tomes from book fairs and auctions and Oxfam shops. We've run out of shelves. We've even run out of floor. We've got piles and piles of books in every room and you have to zig-zag around them carefully or you cause a bookquake. If you have ever been attacked by fifty or a hundred very hard hardbacks then you'll know this is to be avoided at all costs. There are big boxes

of books upstairs too that Dad hasn't even properly sorted. Sometimes you have to climb right over them to get somewhere vital like the toilet.

Gran keeps moaning that the floorboards won't stand up to all that weight. They do tend to creak a bit. Dad gets fussed then and agrees it's ridiculous and sometimes when we're a bit strapped for cash he loads a few boxes into our old car and takes them to a second-hand bookshop to sell. He does sell them too – but he nearly always comes back with another lot of bargains, books he couldn't possibly resist.

Then Gran has another fierce nag and Dad goes all shifty, but when he brings her a big carrier of blockbuster romances from a boot fair she softens up considerably. Gran likes to sit in her special chair with lots of plumped-up cushions at her back, her little legs propped up on her pouffe, a box of Cadbury's Milk Tray wedged in beside her, and a juicy love story in her lap. They're sometimes very *rude*, and when Garnet and I read over her shoulder she swats us away, saying we'll find out something we shouldn't. Ho ho. We found it all out *ages* ago.

Dad reads great fat books too, but they're not modern, they're all classics – Charles Dickens and Thomas Hardy. If we have a look at Dad's book we wonder what the Dickens they're on about and they seem *very* Hardy, but Dad likes them. He also likes boys' adventure books – really old ones where the boys wear knickerbockers and talk like twits: 'I say, old bean', and 'Truly spiffing', and 'Tophole'.

Garnet likes old books too – stuff like *Little Women* and *What Katy Did* and all those E. Nesbit books. And she reads twin books too. Books like *The Twins at St Clare's*. And all the *Sweet Valley Twins*. I read them too, because you can read them nice and quickly. But the books *I* like best are true stories about flashy famous people. Actors and actresses. I skip everything boring and just read the best bits when they're on telly and making movies and all over the front of the newspapers, very flashy and very famous.

We're going to be famous too someday, you bet. So I've started writing our life-story already.

Pearl adores her wild sister. But will life at their new school tear them apart?

MY SISTER JODIE

Jodie. It was the first word I ever said. Most babies lisp *Mumma* or *Dadda* or *Drinkie* or *Teddy*. Maybe everyone names the thing they love best. I said *Jodie*, my sister. OK, I said *Dodie* because I couldn't say my Js properly, but I knew what I meant.

I said her name first every morning.

'Jodie? Jodie! Wake up. *Please* wake up!'

She was hopeless in the mornings. I always woke up early – six o'clock, sometimes even earlier. When I was little, I'd delve around my bed to find my three night-time teddies, and then take them for a dawn trek up and down my duvet. I put my knees up and they'd clamber up the mountain and then slide down. Then they'd burrow back to base camp and tuck into their pretend porridge for breakfast.

I wasn't allowed to eat anything so early. I wasn't even allowed to get up. I was fine once I could read. Sometimes I got through a whole book before the alarm went off. Then I'd lie staring at the ceiling, making up my own stories. I'd wait as long as I could, and then I'd climb into Jodie's bed and whisper her name, give her a little shake and start telling her the new story. They were always about two sisters. They went through an old wardrobe into a magic land, or they went to stage school and became famous actresses, or they went to a ball in beautiful long dresses and danced in glass slippers.

It was always hard to get Jodie to wake up properly. It was as if she'd fallen down a long dark tunnel in the night. It took her ages to crawl back to the surface. But eventually she'd open one eye and her arm went round me automatically. I'd cuddle up and carry on telling her the story. I had to keep nudging her and saying, 'You *are* still awake, aren't you, Jodie?'

'I'm wide awake,' she mumbled, but I had to give her little prods to make sure.

When she *was* awake, she'd sometimes take over the story. She'd tell me how the two sisters ruled over the magic land as twin queens, and they acted in their own daily television soap, and they danced with each other all evening at the ball until way past midnight.

Jodie's stories were always much better than mine. I begged her to write them down but she couldn't be bothered.

'*You* write them down for me,' she said. 'You're the one that wants to be the writer.'

I wanted to write my own stories and illustrate them too.

'I can help you with the ideas,' said Jodie. 'You can do all the drawings and I'll do the colouring in.'

'So long as you do it carefully in the right

colours,' I said, because Jodie nearly always went over the lines, and sometimes she coloured faces green and hair blue just for the fun of it.

'OK, Miss Picky,' said Jodie. 'I'll help you out but that won't be my *real* job. I'm going to be an actress. That's what I really want to do. Imagine, standing there, all lit up, with everyone listening, hanging on your every word!'

'Maybe one of my stories could be turned into a play and then you could have the star part.'

'Yeah, I'll be an overnight success and be offered mega millions to make movies and we'll live together in a huge great mansion,' said Jodie.

'What does a mansion look like?' I said. 'Can it have towers? Can our room be right at the top of a tower?'

'*All* the rooms are our rooms, but we'll share a very special room right at the top of a tower, only I'm not going to let you grow your hair any longer.' She pulled one of my plaits. 'I don't want you tossing it out of the window and letting any wicked old witches climb up it.' Jodie nudged me. She had started to have a lot of arguments with our mother. She often called her a witch – or worse – but only under her breath.

'Don't worry, I'll keep my plaits safely tied up. No access for wicked witches,' I said, giggling, though I felt a bit mean to Mum.

'What about handsome princes?'

'*Definitely* not,' I said. 'It'll be just you and me in Mansion Towers, living happily ever after.'

It was just our silly early-morning game, though I took it more seriously than Jodie. I drew our imaginary mansion, often slicing it open like a doll's house so I could illustrate every room. I gave us a huge black velvet sofa with two big black toy pumas lolling at either end. We had two real black cats for luck lapping from little bowls in the kitchen, two poodles curled up together in their dog basket, while twin black ponies grazed in a paddock beside our rose garden. I coloured each rose carefully and separately, deep red, salmon, peach, very pale pink, apricot and yellow. I even tried to do every blade of grass individually but had to see sense after dabbing delicately for half an hour, my hand aching.

I gave us a four-poster bed with red velvet curtains and a ruby chandelier, and one wall was a vast television screen. We had a turquoise swimming pool in the basement (with our twin pet dolphins) and a roof garden between the towers where skylarks and bluebirds skimmed the blossom trees.

I printed the title of each of our books in the library in weeny writing and drew every item of food on our kitchen shelves. I gave us a playroom with a trampoline and a trapeze and a jukebox, and one of those machines you get at the seaside where you have to manoeuvre a crane to pick up little furry teddies. I drew tiny teddies every colour of the rainbow, and I had a shelf of big teddies in our bedroom, and a shelf of old-fashioned dolls with real hair and glass eyes, and a splendid rocking horse big enough for both of us to ride on.

I talked about it to Jodie as if we'd really live there one day. Sometimes I imagined it so vividly it seemed like a real place. I just had to work out which road to take out of town and then I'd round a corner and spot the towers. I'd run fast, through the elaborate wrought-iron gates, up to the front door with the big lion's-head knocker. I'd know how to press the lion's snout with my finger and the door would spring open and I'd step inside and Jodie would be there waiting for me.

I wasn't stupid, I knew it wasn't really real, but it felt as if it might be all the same.

Then one morning at breakfast everything changed. I was sitting at the kitchen table nibbling at a honey sandwich. I liked opening the sandwich up and licking the honey, letting it ooze over my tongue, but I did it quickly and furtively when Mum wasn't looking. She was very strict about table manners. She was forever nagging Jodie about sitting up straight and spooning her cornflakes up quietly without clanking the spoon against the bowl. Jodie slumped further into an S shape and clanked until she nearly cracked the china. Mum took hold of her by the shoulders and gave her a good shaking.

'Stop winding me up, you contrary little whatsit,' she said, going *shake shake shake*.

Jodie's head rocked backwards and forwards on her stiff shoulders.

'You're hurting her!' said Dad, putting down his *Daily Express* and looking anxious.

'She's not hurting me,' Jodie gasped, waggling her head herself, and then she started da-da-da-ing part of that weird old 'Bohemian Rhapsody' song when everyone bangs their heads to the music.

'Stop that silly row! I suppose you think you're funny,' said Mum.

But Dad was laughing and shaking his own

head. 'You're a right head-case, our Jodie,' he said.

'Trust you to encourage her, Joe,' said Mum. 'Why do you always have to take Jodie's side?'

'Because I'm my daddy's girl,' said Jodie, batting her eyelashes at Dad.

She was too. She was always in trouble now, bunking off school and staying out late. Mum could shake her head until it snapped right off her shoulders but she couldn't control her. But Dad could still sometimes make her hang her head and cry because she'd worried them so.

He'd never say a bad word against Jodie.

'It's not her fault. OK, she's always been a bit headstrong, but she's basically been a good little kid. She's just got in with the wrong crowd now, that's all. She's no worse than any of her mates at school,' he said.

'Quite!' said Mum. 'Moorcroft's a rubbish school. The kids aren't taught properly at all. They just run wild. Half of them are in trouble with the police. It was the biggest mistake in the world letting our Jodie go there. She's heading for trouble in a big way. Just *look* at her!'

I thought Jodie looked wonderful. She used to have pale mousy hair in meek little plaits but now she'd dyed her hair a dark orangy-red with streaky gold bits. She wore it in a funny spiky ponytail with a fringe she'd cut herself. Dad said she looked like a pot of marmalade – he'd spread her on toast if she didn't watch out. Mum said Jodie had ruined her hair and now she looked tough and tarty. Jodie was thrilled. She *wanted* to look tough and tarty.

Then there were her ears. Jodie had been begging Mum to let her have her ears pierced. Mum always said no, so last year Jodie went off and got her ears pierced herself. She kept going back, so there are five extra little rings up one ear.

'You've got more perforations than a blooming colander,' said Dad.

Mum was outraged at each and every new piercing.

'Hey, hey, they're only pretty little earrings,' said Dad. 'It's not as if she's got a nose-stud or a tattoo.'

'*Yet*!' Jodie whispered to me.

She'd tried going to a tattoo parlour but they said she was too young. She inked butterflies and blue-birds and daisy chains up and down her arms and legs with my felt pens instead. She looked incredible in her underwear with her red-gold hair and her earrings and her fake tattoos – but her clothes were mostly as dull and little-girly as mine. Jodie didn't have enough money to buy much herself. Mum was in charge when it came to clothes-buying. Dad didn't dare slip Jodie some money any more. She'd told him this story about her clunky school shoes rubbing her toes sore, so he gave her forty pounds for some new ones. She bought her first pair of proper high heels, fantastic flashy sparkly red shoes, and clacked happily round the house in them, deaf to Mum's fury. She let me try them out. They were so high I immediately fell over, twisting my ankle, but I didn't care. I felt like Dorothy wearing her ruby slippers in *The Wizard of Oz*.

Jodie was wearing the clunky school shoes this morning, and the grey Moorcroft uniform. She'd done her best to customize it, hitching up the skirt as high as she could, and she'd pinned funny badges on her blazer. She'd inked little cartoon characters all over her school tie. Mum started on a new nag about the tie, but she interrupted herself when she heard the letterbox bang.

'Post, Pearl. Go and get it, pet.'

I'm Pearl. When I was born, Mum called me her precious little pearl and the name stuck. I was born prematurely and had to stay tucked up in an incubator for more than a month. I only weighed a kilo and was still so little when they were allowed to bring me home that Dad could cradle me in one of his hands. They were very worried about Jodie's reaction to me. She was a harem-scarem little girl who always twisted off her dolls' heads and kicked her teddies – but she was incredibly careful with me. She held me very gently and kissed my little wrinkled forehead and stroked my fluffy hair and said I was the best little sister in the whole world.

Sisters appear in Jacky's books all the time! Here's a fun quiz to test your knowledge.

1. In *Clean Break*, what is Em's little sister called?

2. Who threatens to name her new baby stepsister Ethel?

3. Name all the Diamond Girls.

4. Who is Pippa and Hank's joke-telling big sister?

5. What school do sisters Pearl and Jodie go to?

6. Which famous twins do Ruby and Garnet audition to play in *Double Act*?

7. In *Lily Alone*, Baxter has three sisters – name them all!

8. Name the sisters whose unusual mum is called Marigold.

9. Who has a very difficult brother named Will?

10. In *Little Darlings*, what's the name of Destiny's secret sister?

1. Vita **2.** Andy **3.** Dixie, Rochelle, Jude and Martine **4.** Elsa
5. Melchester College **6.** The Twins at St Clare's **7.** Lily, Bliss and Pixie
8. Dolphin and Star **9.** Violet **10.** Sunset

There are oodles of incredible Jacqueline Wilson books to enjoy! Tick off the ones you have read, so you know which ones to look for next!

- ☐ THE DINOSAUR'S PACKED LUNCH
- ☐ THE MONSTER STORY-TELLER
- ☐ THE CAT MUMMY
- ☐ LIZZIE ZIPMOUTH
- ☐ SLEEPOVERS
- ☐ BAD GIRLS
- ☐ THE BED AND BREAKFAST STAR
- ☐ BEST FRIENDS
- ☐ BIG DAY OUT
- ☐ BURIED ALIVE!
- ☐ CANDYFLOSS
- ☐ CLEAN BREAK
- ☐ CLIFFHANGER
- ☐ COOKIE
- ☐ THE DARE GAME
- ☐ THE DIAMOND GIRLS
- ☐ DOUBLE ACT
- ☐ GLUBBSLYME
- ☐ HETTY FEATHER
- ☐ THE ILLUSTRATED MUM
- ☐ JACKY DAYDREAM
- ☐ LILY ALONE
- ☐ LITTLE DARLINGS
- ☐ LOLA ROSE
- ☐ THE LONGEST WHALE SONG
- ☐ THE LOTTIE PROJECT
- ☐ MIDNIGHT
- ☐ THE MUM-MINDER
- ☐ SAPPHIRE BATTERSEA
- ☐ SECRETS
- ☐ STARRING TRACY BEAKER
- ☐ THE STORY OF TRACY BEAKER
- ☐ THE SUITCASE KID
- ☐ VICKY ANGEL
- ☐ THE WORRY WEBSITE
- ☐ THE WORST THING ABOUT MY SISTER

FOR OLDER READERS:

- ☐ DUSTBIN BABY
- ☐ GIRLS IN LOVE
- ☐ GIRLS IN TEARS
- ☐ GIRLS OUT LATE
- ☐ GIRLS UNDER PRESSURE
- ☐ KISS
- ☐ LOVE LESSONS
- ☐ MY SECRET DIARY
- ☐ MY SISTER JODIE